SHOOT THE GAP

NELSON HIGH RAIDERS #4

JORDAN FORD

BONUS GOODIES

If you're like me and you love to know how the author pictures the characters, then you're welcome to check out my Pinterest board for this series. Just click the link below:

https://www.pinterest.nz/melissapearlauthor/a-big-play-novels/

And if you'd like to sign up for my latest news, exclusive offers, plus receive a free introduction to the Ryder Bay series, then just **FOLLOW THIS LINK...**

https://www.subscribepage.com/JF_book_signup

———

www.jordanfordbooks.com

For Peter — the guy I'd do anything for. The one who can make me laugh the hardest and smile the biggest. Thank you for being the love of my life and my best friend.

LOOKING FOR THE PERFECT FINISH

TYLER

IN LESS THAN TWO MONTHS, school's about to change for good. I'm still trying to decide how I feel about that. Flicking my skateboard up, I catch it with my hand and rest it against my hip as I walk the last few feet into school. I spot Mack's Camaro in its usual spot next to Colt's truck.

Can't believe they won't be here next year. It kind of sucks. I have to end this year well and head into *my* senior year as the guy people are talking about, the one they want to be like. It'll take away the sting of losing my pals. Besides, I'm sick of people saying my name and scoffing, *yeah, that clown.* I want them to say Tyler Schumann with this awe-inspired smile on their faces because, for once, I'm the hero.

I'm still trying to figure out how to make that happen, but I have to do it fast because I'm running out of time to win over one particular senior. Oh man, scoring with her would make me a freaking legend at this school. The smile that comes over me every time I think about Roxanne Carmichael quickly peters out as I climb the front steps.

It's been kind of impossible to get noticed by her, because I'm living in the shadow of legends.

I know those towers won't be blocking me next year, but my rep is kind of established, and after everything that's gone down recently—as in seeing three macho men brought to their knees by chicks I never thought they'd fall for—I'm starting to wonder if I need to change up the sex-god, funny guy routine. Maybe Roxy will notice me if I act more like Mack.

I scan my surroundings, checking out the hotties and raising my chin at Darius, who's locking up his bike next to Sam's BMX. Not sure where she is, but I'll see her in history class. We sit in the back together, mostly goofing off and passing notes and silly cartoons to each other. It's my favorite subject.

"'Sup, Flash!" Some second-string sophomore gives me a high five as he struts past. He'll probably be promoted to first string next season, so I should really learn his name. I've never been great with names. I should probably work on that.

If I'm going to be filling the shoes of guys like Mack and Colt, there's a lot of things I need to work on. There's just this one itty-bitty, major problem.

"Hey, man, how's it going?"

I glance up to find Colt smiling at me. I grin back, trying to ignore how much I'm going to miss him. I shouldn't even be thinking past tomorrow, anyway.

Enjoy the moment, right?

I bump my fist against his and wink at Tori, who's tucked beneath his arm. She's going low-key today in a pair of skinny jeans and a plaid shirt, but those bands are still all over her wrists and she's got a daisy flower clip on the side of her head, not to mention her home-made patchwork satchel. I have to admit, she's grown on me big time. I didn't want to like her at first. I was worried she'd bring with her an army of nerds who'd take over our table in the cafeteria. Not to sound like a prick, but smart-ass know-it-alls like Anderson Foster do my head in.

Thankfully, the nerd squad stuck to their own turf and although Tori's smart, she doesn't shove it in anyone's face. Her little quirks and speed-talking are actually kind of cute, and she lets me hassle her without getting all girly about it.

Running her little fingers through her untamed curls, she grins up at me and wrinkles her nose.

"What?" I draw out the word, already wary of her answer.

"You smell like you took a bath in cologne this morning." She pinches her nose while Colt snickers.

I narrow my eyes into a dry glare. "Yeah, well, prom season is upon us and if I'm going to score a hot date, I need to smell good."

"True." She nods with a grimace. "But you don't want them passing out from the overpowering fumes before they're able to say yes, right? Unless that's a new tactic you're going for. You know, they faint, you catch them, and as you kiss them awake, say something smooth like, 'Thanks for saying yes, baby. I'm going to show you the night of your life.'"

I don't know who the hell she's trying to mimic with that voice. It sure as shit better not be me.

I try to keep my glare intact, but the expression on her face is freaking adorkable and I know I'm going to crack a smile soon.

I huff and flick a thumb over my shoulder. "You know what, just keep walking, sweetheart. I'll catch your nerdy little butt later."

Tori giggles while Colt sends me one of his standard looks of warning. I know I'm not supposed to call his girl a nerd, but we're just joking around. Geez, the guy is overprotective. I roll my eyes at him and saunter away, sniffing my shoulder.

Okay, so it's strong but it's not that bad.

In truth, I hadn't meant to put quite so much on, but my little sister, Shiloh, barged into the bathroom, scaring the shit out of me and making me spill half the bottle on myself. I was already running late and didn't have time to change. I'd hoped that skating to school might help air me out a bit. Obviously not.

Turning the corner, I head to my locker and am stopped by a familiar sight. Tank's tall ass is blocking my space as he hovers beside his girlfriend, leaning against my locker door and acting like the rest of the world is invisible. Yeah, they're a little tongue-tied right now.

As much as I want to roll my eyes again, I can't help smirking, especially when Layla has to rise to her tiptoes to deepen the kiss. She's such a midget beside him. Yet again, let cuteness prevail. Between her and Tori, they've got the word nailed. I never thought I'd see this side of Layla. She's always been so cool and aloof, but Finn's awakened something inside of her, and we're all catching glimpses of the kid I remember from elementary school. The happy one who used to skip to school with a confident smile and giggle at practically everything.

Finn's been a happy boy since scoring the hot little cheerleader, and now that Mack's cool with the situation, things have been going pretty well for everyone.

"No, but Lauren told me the fight all started because Layla's stepbrother tried to kiss her."

"Ew. Why did he do that?"

I flinch at the female voices behind me. I shouldn't be doing that anymore. After three weeks of gossip, you'd think I'd be used to hearing my friends' names bashed around, but I'm not. I don't think I ever will be, because I hate hearing the derisive tone that always accompanies the chatter.

"Who knows."

"So Finn takes a beating for it? That's so wrong."

"I know, right? She probably came onto her stepbrother and he just went with it. It's not like they're related by blood or anything, but still...so creepy. Finn would have been super pissed. Totally unfair that such a nice guy has to put up with her shit all the time."

My scowl deepens, but I'm not ready to turn around and stop them. The school's been kind of divided since Layla and Finn got together. People's true opinions have risen to the surface, especially when everyone found out about the fight by the lake.

"Do you honestly think she would do that?"

"You know what she's like. What's the bet she got drunk off her ass and sent all the wrong messages to that asshole? And then Finn ends up getting hurt trying to defend her."

I snap my eyes shut, clenching my jaw as the anger inside of me grows from a simmer to a boil. These prissy little girls behind me don't know jack. Okay, so maybe Layla put herself in a really stupid position, but according to her, she had no idea what she was doing, and we all underestimated Derek's psychopathic tendencies. I still want to strangle the guy for hitting her. Any man who lays a hand on a girl like that is a total asshole in my book. There's no excuse to ever hit a girl. Ever.

"Why is it that the best-looking guys have to be the stupidest, as well?" The girl behind me sighs. "First Mack goes and falls for that chick who murdered someone, and now one of the nicest guys on the team falls for a slut-bag."

That's it.

I spin around and fling back the locker door they've been gossiping behind. They both gasp and stare up at me with large eyes. I recognize them both, but of course can't remember their names. The one with the big-ass camera around her neck is a senior and hangs out with Anderson Foster. The other one, I'm not sure what grade she's in, but I hope it's twelfth so she can be gone by the end of the year.

"H-hey, Tyler." Camera girl gives me a weak smile.

My only response is to shake my head and give them a glare that tells them I heard everything. They look at each other with nervous titters, then snatch up their bags. I slam the girl's locker shut for her and they scamper away from me. The sound shoots down the hallway, bringing all eyes on me.

Finn looks over Layla's head with a quizzical frown. I paste on a friendly grin and tip my fingers at him. He doesn't need to know the crap I just heard. Layla's still pretty sensitive over the whole thing, and she has every right to be.

Those photos of her, Derek and Quaid are nasty. I struggled to look at them and I can only imagine how the school will react if those pics ever see the light of day.

We can't let that happen. The party paparazzo is still out there somewhere. We haven't spoken about it much, all preferring to pretend like it's not a real threat, but we're lying to ourselves. Any day now, we could walk into this school and find dirty images plastered along the walls.

Layla wouldn't cope, and Finn would be so damn riled. Crossing my arms, I watch the pair head away from Layla's locker. Her thin arm is around his waist, her long hair spilling over her shoulder as she looks up at him. He's saying something that's making her smile, and I catch a glimpse of unchecked Layla again. She's beautiful.

Heading to my locker, I yank it open and cram my board inside. Resting my hands on the metal edge, I stare into the dark space until my eyes lose focus.

I can't just sit back and let this slide. One of us has to do something, and if I'm wanting hero status by the end of the year, then it's got to be me. A slow smile tugs at my lips as I picture myself finding the culprit and ridding the world of those photos, telling Layla it's all good, because I, Tyler Schumann, saved the day. The guys would have no choice but to be totally impressed by me, and Roxy would think I was the bomb for saving her best friend.

"Yeah, I'm liking that," I murmur. Nodding, I step back and close my locker before strutting off to homeroom.

This will be the perfect opportunity to prove to everyone that I'm not just some idiot guy who wears too much cologne and talks a big game. I want to show them that I can *be* big game. That I can be the one to give all of them the perfect ending they're looking for.

My mind starts to run with ideas of where to start. It quickly gets clogged as my scattered thoughts merge together. I may need a little help pulling this off...and there's only one person, outside my usual crew, that I trust enough to be my sidekick.

Sammy Carmichael.

2

AN IRRESISTIBLE INVITATION

SAMMY

CHEERLEADING practice is always so entertaining.

I snicker and shake my head. Oh man, I can't even think that without scoffing. Leaning against the handlebars of my bike, I gaze over the wire fence and watch the swishing ponytails and shoulder-high kicks. I don't even know how they get their legs that high. Seems unnatural to me.

Okay, yes, these practices entertain me, but not because I like watching a bunch of hot girls shake their booties and pretend like they're the most beautiful people on the planet.

I just can't seem to help stopping and staring at them every time I leave school. It's like a car wreck. I can't *not* watch. They prance around on the grass like My Little Ponies, clapping and giggling. Roxy is front and center, of course. My sister knows how to draw the eye.

My gaze travels down her perfect body. She's wearing bright pink hot pants and a skimpy top that shows off everything. The guys running laps behind her keep checking out her ass every time they pass. I bet she knows it too. She's looking pretty damn triumphant as she calls 'The Plastics' into order.

"Ready, okay!"

I roll my eyes as they run through one of their chants. Their movements are sharp and in sync. Which they should be. They practice like all the time!

"Go, Raiders!" Michelle punches the air and jumps on her tiptoes. Her blonde ponytail swings like a pendulum as she prances on her feet.

Blech. So plastic.

I scan the group, checking out faces and wondering which smiles are actually genuine. They're all trying so hard to impress my sister, no doubt worried that if they don't they'll have hell to pay. I'm so sick of the way people behave around her. She's a freaking human being. That's it. She poops just like anybody else and last I smelled, it wasn't perfume-infused.

I hate the way people do that, treat some like they're more important than others.

Shaking my head with a scoff, I turn to leave but am stopped by the sight of Dana Foster. She's jogging around the track, slowly plodding along. Her face is bright red, with sweat patches already forming on her T-shirt.

I'm surprised she's gone out for track. I was sure she would have been after a coveted position on the cheerleading squad. Man, the amount of times we'd find her hovering by her mailbox just so she could catch a glimpse of Roxy when she left the house was unbelievable.

"Hey, Roxy!" Her irritating little chirp is embedded in my brain. Talk about a girl-crush. She has always acted like a little puppy dog around my sister.

But not anymore.

My eyes narrow as I study her. The short girl puffs past my sister, obviously concentrating on keeping her gaze ahead. I can tell by the set of her jaw that she's aware of Roxy. She starts blinking, her nose twitching just a touch as she runs past. There's no chirping or friendly smile, just this tightening of her lips.

Why the change?

That's what I want to know.

Layla moves into view, flicking her ponytail over her shoulder. She glances at Dana as she runs past. Roxy tips her head at the track and makes some comment. I can tell by her smirk that it's a mean one. I scowl at my nasty sister, pleased when Layla doesn't laugh or snicker. She just looks at Roxy and shakes her head. I love how much she's chilled since hooking up with the Finn-ster. Those two are good together.

I'm still not sure exactly what went down. The fight at the lake sounded kind of intense. I wish I could have been there to do some beating of my own. Guys who hit girls are scum. Tyler hasn't told me everything, but by the sound of it, Layla got some kind of feisty Catwoman routine going and made Derek *Dickman* bleed. She's gone up a few notches in my book because of that.

I've never really interacted with the guy, but I've seen enough. Those Brownridge Bears players are assbutts. Thank God they've all been put on probation. Hopefully, we won't be seeing them around Nelson any time soon.

My phone dings.

Yanking it out of my back pocket, I check the screen and grin. For some weird reason, I seem to smile any time I get a message from Tyler. Even when it's a bossy-ass one like this.

. . .

Meet me at warehouse.

I punch back a quick *See you in 15* and immediately head off. I'm ashamed to say I'd drop anything for the guy. We've been in school together since second grade and although I'd rather die than refer to him as my bestie, that's exactly what he is. Not that I'll ever admit it.

Don't want anyone hearing girly shit like BFF coming out of my mouth.

Tyler's my boy and I've loved him since... I don't even know when it started. Maybe I always have. And that's a secret that will remain mine for life.

————

Pumping my legs, I speed down the street and take a sharp turn into a narrow back alley. The wind makes my hair fly behind me, and I grin as I spot the stairs coming up. Tugging the bars, I pedal harder and laugh when my bike hits air, swooping over the stairs and landing with a thud. I skid out of the landing and race down the quiet street, heading for the metal fence Tyler and I punched a hole in last year.

The back wheel of my bike grinds through the stone-scattered dirt as I skid to a stop. Dumping my bike in the brown grass, I unclip the thick chain from around my waist and secure my bike around the pole before crawling through the hole. I brush the dirt off my knees and walk around the edge of the warehouse. It's an old building that shut down about two years ago.

The walls are thick, gray concrete with hairline fractures and deep chips. The windows are smashed out, and graffiti dominates huge patches.

I love this place.

Rounding the corner, I spot the unused railway track. The metal is brown with rust, and long grass has sprouted between the railroad ties. My shoes crunch on the pebbles as I jump down and then balance on the metal, extending my arms as I walk along like I'm on some gymnastics beam.

"Stop messing around and get your butt up here, Sammy!" Tyler's standing on the second floor of the warehouse, leaning out one of the broken windows.

I laugh and give him the finger before jumping back up and running into the warehouse. The massive iron door is open enough for me to squeeze through. It takes a second for my eyes to adjust to the dim light inside. Gazing up at the huge metal chains hanging from the ceiling, I focus on the pale light beams that cut across the open space.

With a little sniff, I run for the edge of the wall and climb the metal bars, hoisting myself up to the second story. Tyler's leaning against the wall and watching me with a smile as I brush my hands on my butt and walk towards him.

"So, what's the big hurry, My Ty?"

A few people refer to him as the cocktail drink *mai tai*. I don't know when the trend started, but whenever I call him that I'm always thinking *my Ty*. Yet another secret I'll take to the grave.

He clears his throat, crossing his arms and looking unusually serious.

I stop a foot from him, picking up his scent and loving the smell. I'll never say it, but damn, that cologne can do things to my insides. Hot, steamy things.

My nose twitches and I run my finger under it, glancing away so he can't see how much he affects me. I've gotten used to hiding my real emotions around him, but he still catches me off guard sometimes. It's no surprise to me that he's a ladies man. If I were a normal girl, I'd be batting my eyelashes like nobody's business. But that's just not who I am.

Besides, I'll take friendship status over a make-out session any day...or at least most days. I catch myself glancing at his lips and quickly look down to my scuffed Converse.

"I've gotta tell you something." His swallow is loud

enough to pull my gaze from the floor. "It's big, and you gotta promise you won't say a word."

"Come on, man." I give him a pitiful look. "You know you never have to preface that with me. I'm not the gossipy kind."

"Which is why I'm coming to you with this." He perches his butt on the edge of the sill, gripping the chipped wooden frame.

I love his hands. Is that dumb? I just love the length of his fingers, the short nails, the shape of his knuckles. I've watched them change and develop over the last decade, and they've grown into strong, masculine hands. Sexy hands...hands that are holding the sill kind of tight right now, which means this conversation's about to get real.

"Okay." I grab a nearby crate and flip it over to take a seat. "Shoot."

"You know the fight at the lake?"

"Yeah, you told me about it."

He crosses his ankles. "I didn't tell you everything. I didn't tell you why Derek and those guys came after Finn."

Again with the serious look on his face. It's kind of unnerving, but I also really like it. Tyler's letting me in on something big. It's just one more thing to make our relationship stronger.

I hide my glee by pressing my lips together and looking down at my worn sneaks. "I just assumed they were being assholes."

"Why do you think Layla bit his lip?"

I shrug. "Because he was trying to kiss her."

He nods. "Yeah."

His grim expression makes my stomach knot with foreboding. "What aren't you saying? Did Layla and Derek hook up for real?"

Tyler's heavy sigh tells me everything I need to know. I grimace and resist the urge to dry-wretch. That's seriously gross. Anyone getting it on with that weasel is disgusting, but the whole sibling thing just adds a new ick factor that's super creepy.

"There's photos, Sam."

"What?" My eyes pop so wide I'm waiting for them to fall out of their sockets.

"Layla got completely wasted at this party and got it on with Derek and Quaid. There's photos. I've seen them."

I'm so stunned it takes me a moment of slow blinking to actually respond. "I keep hearing these rumors about

Derek trying to kiss Layla, but I didn't think she was into it. That's why she bit him, right?"

"It was before then. The lake fight happened after she exposed the photos to her family. Derek got in deep shit with his dad, and he wanted payback."

"So, wait a second." I scrub a hand over my face. "You're telling me that Layla had a little threesome going on with those scumbags and there's photographic evidence?"

Tyler's head bobs once, a short sharp movement to match the set of his jaw. "Derek tried to blackmail her with the pictures, but we stole them off his computer and—"

"Stop." I raise my hand in the air. "Who's 'we'?"

"Finn, Colt and me."

My forehead wrinkles with a disgruntled frown. "You broke into his place and stole stuff off his computer?"

Tyler nods.

"Dude!" I fling my hands wide. "How could you not invite me to be a part of that? That sounds awesome."

Tyler shoots me a dry glare. "Come on, Sam. It's not like I could tell anyone. Finn would kick my ass. We have to keep this on the down-low."

"Well, tell me about it now. How'd you get in? Was

there an alarm or anything?" I point at him. "Did you do it at like four o'clock in the morning? Because that's the best time to break into someone's place."

A smile tugs at the edge of Tyler's mouth and he nods, quickly explaining how Colt climbed in the garage window and unlocked the back door for them. They nearly got busted by Derek's mom and had to scramble out his bedroom window.

"Man," I kind of whine. "That would have been epic."

He snickers and winks at me. "I'll invite you next time, 'kay?"

"I'm guessing you're hoping there won't be a next time."

"Pretty much."

I give in with a half-scowl that soon morphs into a reluctant smile. I can't stay mad at that face—that gorgeous face with its dark eyebrows and full lips. He's starting to get faint stubble above his lip and on his chin now too. As soon as I start wondering how prickly or soft it feels, I shift my gaze to the ground and spot a stone near my foot. Snatching it up, I start tossing it in the air and catching it again. "So, why are you telling me now?"

Gripping the back of his neck, Tyler pops up straight and starts pacing. "The person who took those photos is still out there, and according to Layla, he goes to Nelson High."

"No way," I whisper, a little thrill racing through me. I love a good mystery. "How does she know that?"

"Derek implied it."

"So it could be a lie."

"What if it's not?" Tyler spins to face me. "What if that party paparazzo is lurking the halls of Nelson High waiting to pounce? I have to find out who it is and stop him before he can use those photos against her. Derek might not be a threat anymore, but someone else still could be. It only takes one little cartoon to wipe someone out, remember?"

We share a sad smile. My gut pinches as I think of Kiwi Girl. I really liked her. And the way she left totally sucked.

"Okay." I stand, pinching my bottom lip as I start to pace beside him. "So, what have you done so far?"

"Nothing. Everyone's so busy trying to squash the lake fight rumors that they're not talking about it. It's like we're all pretending that the photos don't exist anymore. But they do, and if they surface, all that gossip we're trying to ignore is going to be proven correct. People are getting too close to the truth, and I don't think we should be giving them any more ammo.

Our threatening glares when we hear people gossiping are only gonna go so far. We won't be able to counter the truth if it's exposed."

My shoes scuff through the dust as I spin and head back towards Tyler. A little shiver races down my spine as I picture Layla playing tonsil hockey with that jerk-off Derek. So gross.

Tyler catches my eye and I stop pacing. The way the light is cast over his face right now, it makes his eyes this cool teal color. I want to dive right into them and go skinny-dipping.

"That's why I need you." He tips his chin at me.

Damn, I love those words. I swallow to counter the smile busting to break free.

"The guys probably won't want me going after this. They'll no doubt think I'm stirring up trouble, but I can't stand around doing nothing." He crosses his arms, making his biceps look that much bigger. "So, what do you think? You want to play spies with me?"

It's the best invitation I've ever heard. I don't even have to say yes; I just give him a big smile and he knows exactly what I'm thinking.

This is going to be legendary.

3

IMAGINE IF SHE SAID YES

TYLER

PLAYING SPIES.

It sounds so lame, but the grin on Sammy's face made it totally worth it. I'm glad I brought her in. She's always been the friend I can trust with anything. With her whole anti-cliques mentality, it makes her a pretty safe bet. She's not going to skate off and gossip to anyone. I really love that about her.

Sauntering into the school, I tip my chin at the hottie with the strawberry-blonde curls. Sasha? No, Sarah. Maybe Sonia? Aw, crap, I'm bad with names.

I settle for "Hey, beautiful" as I saunter past.

Her freckled cheeks flare red and she dips her head, but

I can't help wondering if she's rolling her eyes behind my back.

I'm not stupid. I can read body language. I know what people think about me. I wish I could turn off the façade sometimes, but every time I step into school it just comes over me and I'm not sure how to stop it.

"Hey, man." Mack appears on my left, stepping in time with me as I head to my locker. Layla's beside him, busy on her phone.

"'Sup, Mack-Attack?"

"Nothin' much." He shrugs. I kind of miss his cocky swagger. It was stolen by Kaija…or at least the events that led to her sudden departure. He's still every bit as cool as he used to be, and definitely happier since hooking back up with Kaija in New Zealand, but he's a toned-down version of what he once was. There's a maturity about him now that's trampled his player charm. It makes me wonder which version of Mack I should be aspiring to.

He nudges my arm as we round the corner. "You good, man?"

"Yeah." I nod and look away from him. I should probably tell him that I'm after the guy who took those photos of his sister, but I can't bring myself to do it. I'm not sure if he'll tell me to back off or want in on the action.

I don't like either option.

One, I don't like ignoring the guy's wishes and secondly, if he wants in, he'll steal all my glory, and I'm not in a sharing mood over this one. If I'm going to redesign my rep at this school, I have to be the hero. Besides, after the way each of my friends has fought for their ladies, I feel like I need to step it up if I'm going to win over a princess like Roxy. She deserves a shining knight. And it's going to be me.

A freshman with glossy black hair and a cute smile catches my eye. I wink at her and grin when she hides her smile behind her binder. I glance back to find Mack giving me a pitiful headshake.

"What?" I snap and point over my shoulder. "A few months ago, you would have been doing exactly the same thing."

Layla looks up from her phone. "Doing what?"

"Nothing," we answer in unison.

Layla tucks her phone into her bag and rolls her eyes. "See you guys later." Her boots clip on the floor as she struts away. I like the way her long hair bounces on her shoulders as she walks. My gaze travels down her shapely body until I get smacked in the chest with the back of Mack's hand.

"Oof!" I rub the sore spot. "I'm just admiring the beauty of God's crea—"

"Shut it," Mack cuts me off. "You think Finn's going to appreciate you checking out his girl?"

"It's not like I'm into her. I was just…" I finish with a huff. "Whatever."

Mack smirks at me. "Dude, you need to score your own girl. Stop wasting your time with these one-night stands and get serious already."

"Are you crazy? I'm seventeen years old. I'm not getting serious. Just because you guys are all whipped doesn't mean I need to be."

"Have it your way." Mack shrugs. "But I'm telling you, man, whipped is not as bad as it sounds." The dreamy look in his eyes is just a little too mushy for my tastes.

I stick out my tongue and make a gagging noise. I may want to be the knight and all that, but I'm not about to be a whipped one.

Mack laughs and lightly punches my arm. "You just wait, man. When you eventually find that girl, you're gonna be in so much trouble."

"Not gonna happen." I shake my head with a confident smirk that stays in place until he turns away from me.

If only he knew the truth. One-night stands? Oh man, he has no idea.

I pull my shoulders back, hoping the stress lines in my façade aren't showing.

We round the corner and instead of splitting to head for my locker, I stick with Mack. Something at the end of the hall has caught my eye. For once, it's not some hot chick. Well, I mean it kind of is. Ricco is taking snapshots of some of the cheerleaders. They're standing in a cute little bunch, looking hot and adorable in the same moment with their shapely bodies and shining smiles.

The grin on Ricco's face is pretty funny. No wonder he signed up to be part of the yearbook committee.

But, see, my heart's racing right now. I can't take my eyes off my buddy and the way his fingers are curled around the body of the camera.

"That's it, girls. Just a few more shots!"

One of the girls shouts, "Roxy for prom queen!" They all cheer and laugh while Ricco snaps away, capturing the camaraderie and energy among the girls.

As he holds his finger on the button, I'm transported to a party scene where Mack's little sister is being felt up by two Brownridge Bears players. Ricco grins at the display screen and gets snappy-happy.

Anger fires through me. I force a blink and bring myself back to the Nelson High hallway. Was it him? A Raider? One of the offensive team, someone I've been running with for years?

I grip the strap of my bag, trying to talk myself out of the swift conclusion, but my brain's in hunt-down mode and the guy fits the bill. He parties, he likes to take photos, and like me, he likes to check out the hotties any chance he gets.

Ricco lowers the camera and beams at the girls. "Thank you, ladies."

They grin and go their separate ways, obviously aware of how gorgeous they are. Ricco checks out the shots he's just taken, looking triumphant. He glances up and smiles at me, but the look quickly disappears behind a confused frown. I must still be glaring at him. Forcing my expression out of a scowl, I paste on a smile and raise my chin.

He gives me one more confused frown before shaking his head and walking away, his eyes glued to his camera screen. I need to get my hands on that thing and go through it. I don't like the idea of spying on one of my teammates, but if I have to take him down to keep Layla safe from exposure then that's what I'm going to do.

I'm about to say goodbye to Mack and subtly follow

Ricco when the school's hottest female distracts me. She's strutting towards us in her pale pink skirt and a skintight T-shirt that has the words *Girl Power* stretching over her breasts. Damn. She is so freaking fine. Those luscious waves of dark hair that curl past her shoulders, those wide blue eyes, and don't even get me started on her lips. They're full and totally suckable. She's been smokin' hot ever since hitting puberty, and I've wanted to score with her since freshman year.

Roxanne Carmichael.

For some reason, her full name always whispers through my head like my brain is sighing it with this dopey smile.

Unfortunately, Roxy's never given me any attention, but that's not going to stop me from trying. Just wait until I out the photo bandit. Surely Layla has told her all about it by now. They're best friends. Once I bring the guy to his knees, word will get to Roxy. She'll have to think I'm epic after that, right?

I swallow, doubts tickling the back of my brain.

Roxy's hips have a little extra sway going as she and Michelle strut up to Mack. Her rippled skirt is short enough to give me a decent view of her smooth skin. I track her perfect legs, loving the way her hot pink Converse come up around her skinny ankles.

"Hey, Mack." Her sultry voice makes my eyes ping back up to her face.

Her skin's like porcelain, milky white and luscious. And those blues eyes... They're like sapphires, man.

I shuffle a little closer so I can get in on Mack's conversation.

Michelle eyes me warily so I put on my best smile. She gives me a bored eye roll and looks to Mack.

I don't care. I'm not interested in her, anyway. Since Colt's been taken off the market, it's become common knowledge that Michelle only dates guys outside of Nelson. Her radar's been reset for college guys, apparently. I'm sure they're loving it.

I track my gaze back to Roxy and the smile on her luscious lips.

"So..." She rests her binder on her hip and flicks a chocolate brown curl over her shoulder. "Prom's not far away, and I figure we should get organized. Now I'm planning on wearing—"

"What are you talking about?" Mack cuts her off.

"Going to prom together." She gives him an incredulous look. "You know we have to, right?"

"No." Mack shakes his head.

Crazy bastard. Why isn't he jumping all over this?

"I'm not going to prom, Rox."

Her head snaps back, her rosebud lips parting in surprise. "Why not?"

"Because I don't have my date."

"*I* will be your date! That's what I'm saying." She taps her perfect chest, raising her eyebrows like it's obvious.

With a heavy sigh, Mack flicks his locker open. "My girl's in New Zealand, and I'm not going without her."

"That's insane! You can't skip prom. She's not going to care if you go with someone else. It's not even a romantic thing. We're obviously going to be crowned king and queen, so it makes sense to go together."

"Well, I'm not going, so Nelson High will just have to find another king." His locker snaps shut.

Roxy's still gaping at him like he's demented, and I'm struggling to find the right words. I can't believe the guy is bailing over a girl. That's so incredibly lame. I'm kind of pissed, to be honest, but I shove my anger aside in order to take advantage of the one and only opportunity I'll probably have.

"I'll take you, Foxy Roxy." I wriggle my eyebrows at her and am rewarded with a soft snicker. Her alluring eyes hit my face and then travel down my body, her lips rising into a sexy little smirk.

Glancing at Mack, she shakes her head and mumbles to Michelle, "Let's go."

They glide past us and I turn to watch them leave, taking a moment to admire Roxy one last time. Scoring that girl would be a wish come true.

Imagine walking into prom with Roxanne Carmichael holding your hand. Now that would be epic.

Too bad I got no more than a smirk. It was better than a sharp frown or a look of disdain, so I'll take it, but man, I would have loved a yes.

4

HAPPY CHAOS

SAMMY

I LEAN my forearms against the fence and thread my fingers together. This is my favorite time of the week. There's no cheerleading practice on Thursdays, so I have an unimpeded view of the running track. And the reason this is so great is because Tyler always trains on Thursdays.

His body glides into view again, running smoothly around the three-quarter turn like it's the easiest thing in the world. He's one of the fastest guys on the football team, and every summer he competes in track, as well. Sprinting is his forte, but today he's loping around the track with music blasting in his ears, obviously doing a little conditioning.

He's shirtless, which helps with the whole eye-candy

factor. Sweat is glistening off his torso and wetting the edges of his hairline. His arms and legs work smoothly together, every toned muscle doing what it should to take him around the bend. The shark tooth necklace his sister gave him last summer bobs against his collarbone. Weird that I'm jealous of a necklace. It makes me lame and pathetic, but I'd love to know what his body feels like, what my fingers would discover if I traced each muscle of his torso then drew a line between his collarbone and over his shoulders. I think about it every time I watch him...then spend the rest of the night torturing myself with the fact I'll never know.

I'm just Sammy, his skate buddy. I'll never be the one to glide my hands over his hard muscles and wrap my arms around his neck while he kisses me. That's not who we are.

Pursing my lips, I push away from the fence. Why do I torture myself like this? When am I going to get it through my thick skull that guys will never look at me the way they look at other girls in my school? I'm not the kind of person you do a double take for...unlike Roxy.

"Hey, sis."

I flinch and pull a face, my shoulders knotting at the sound of my older sister's voice. I keep my eyes on the track, hoping my expression is neutral by the time she reaches me.

"What are you doing here?" She appears beside me. I keep my eyes forward, refusing to look at her or answer her question.

Over my dead body.

I don't know when it started or whether it's always been there, but trusting Roxy has never come naturally to me. We're so different, and it's like we both pride ourselves on remaining that way. She's like Mom and I take after Dad.

I never, ever remember us being close. The only time we do stuff together is when we're forced into family affairs, which suck on too many levels to even explain. Seriously, don't even get me started. It may appear from the outside as though the Carmichaels are this perfect family living in their perfect house, but people don't know the truth.

Roxy's still eyeing me, waiting for my answer.

I shrug and go for super casual. "Just waiting for Tyler to finish up."

Flicking up my skateboard, I catch it with my hand and spin around so my butt's leaning against the fence. I lay the board across my legs and grip the underside, hoping Roxy won't notice. I don't want her seeing anything on my face or body that will give away the fact I've been obsessing over Tyler. He's about to run past again. I hope my expression's bored enough.

The edge of Roxy's mouth tips up, her eyes narrowing at the corners.

Shit.

"Of course you are. You're such a good friend." Her voice is dripping with sickly sweet insincerity.

I clench my jaw, refusing to respond. Out of the corner of my eye, I see her swivel to face the track properly.

"Hmm." Her tone pitches. "He's actually quite hot without a shirt on, isn't he?"

I shrug, but probably not fast enough.

Roxy licks her bottom lip, then pinches it between her teeth. "Yes, indeedy. Some definite eye candy going on there. Not that you've probably noticed. Because you're not into him that way, right?"

I keep my gaze averted, hoping she'll miss the slight flaring of my nostrils.

Her snicker tells me she didn't.

Dammit!

"Well, I wonder what he'd think about that."

I jerk up straight and lean towards her, grateful for my extra couple of inches of height. "I don't like him that way, okay? We're just friends."

Roxy's eyes glimmer with a knowing smile. "Of course you are."

My upper lip curls and I step back, gripping my board against my hip and resisting the urge to smash it into her face. How is it possible that someone related to me can be so damn annoying?

The phone in Roxy's bag dings and about two seconds later, so does mine. I wrench it out of my back pocket and check the screen.

"Oh, great," Roxy moans, no doubt reading the exact same message I am. "Dad's back from his business trip. My night has officially been ruined."

I shove the phone back in my pocket. I'll reply to Mom's message later. Clearing my throat, I step away from the fence and start heading for the path.

"Are you bailing?" Roxy calls out to me.

Dropping the board on the path, I place my foot on it and look at her. "Of course I am."

"Me too. I'm gonna go hang with Michelle." She slides her phone away and gives me a wicked smile. "Hey, maybe you should see if Tyler's free for dinner."

She follows up her wink with an irritating giggle that unsettles my stomach.

Crap. Of all the people in the world to discover me

checking out Tyler, it had to be Roxy. I'm usually so subtle about this kind of thing, but I never expected my sister to pass me on her way out of school. She's usually driving her stupid little car. Why the hell isn't she today?

I push off and skate away from Roxy's grating snicker.

Thanks to her interruption and Mom's text message, I am now in a super foul mood. I'm not about to go home and get stuck at the table with Mom and Dad's tension. Why they haven't just divorced already, I do not know. All I can say is that it was a huge relief when Dad scored his new job last year and started traveling two weeks out of every month.

Tipping my feet, I ease around the corner and aimlessly skate the streets. The minutes tick by and I inevitably find myself heading to Tyler's place. I glance over my shoulder to make sure I'm not being followed by the Roxanator. I wouldn't put it past her.

Satisfied my ride is under the radar, I pick up speed and arrive at Tyler's place ten minutes later. A smile breaches my expression before I'm even aware of it. The Schumann's is only the best house in the entire town of Nelson.

I jump off my board and kick it up, holding it against my side as I lope past the bright blue double garage and around to the front door. As soon as I ring the doorbell, Axel starts barking in the backyard. I grin as I picture the gigantic Great Dane with his big doe eyes and shiny black fur. He's been in the family for four years now and he's the most affectionate dog I've ever met.

"I'm just saying!" Tyler's mom yells over her shoulder as she opens the door. A muffled reply I can't quite hear comes from the back of the house and she starts laughing.

A huge smile spreads across my face before she turns to notice me. I love the way she interacts with her husband. They yell at each other but it's always followed by laughter...unlike my parents.

Her already happy face jumps with surprised pleasure when she looks at me.

"Oh hey! It's my favorite teenager. How you doin', sweetie?" She pulls me into a hug and gives me a big kiss on the cheek.

"Hey, Roma." I know I should be calling her Mrs. Schumann, but I tried that for over a year and it never flew. She won't even settle for Aunt Roma.

"It's Roma. Ro-ma. Seriously, how many times do I have to tell you that?"

I tried to tell her that Mom would kill me if she ever heard me being so casual with one of my friends' parents, but she just grinned and said, *"All the more reason to do it."*

I was eight at the time, and it's safe to say I fell in love with her after that.

"Come in. Come in." She waves her hand, ushering me inside before bending down to pile the rabble of shoes onto the overflowing shoe rack. I lean my skateboard against the wall and jump over the school bag tipped up by the entrance to the living room.

"Shy, come pick up your bag, hon!" Roma calls up the stairs before grinning at me. "Want a drink?"

"Yeah, sure." I nod and walk through the family room, ruffling Braxton's hair as I pass him.

He looks up from the massive picture book in his lap, his face puckering with a bashful smile. I can't believe how much he's grown, even since spring break.

I point over my shoulder and whisper to Roma. "Are four-year-olds supposed to grow that fast?"

Roma laughs, her head popping out from behind the pantry door. "I know, right? He has blossomed so much since we got him. I guess he had some catching up to do." She gives me a meaningful smile.

I glance back into the living room to check out the little boy sitting on the couch. He arrived in the Schumann home about a year ago and was the size of an eighteen-month-old. Adopting him from China had been a real mission, but Roma and Donnie were determined to bring the little guy into their home. They had to shell out for clef palate surgery and pay for a bunch of medical expenses before they were allowed to bring him back to the States. But it's been worth it. The kid has progressed by leaps and bounds.

"Hey, Sammy Dee! What's up?"

I start laughing before I even turn around to face the one member of the family who can always surprise me. Seriously, the way she looks and the stuff that comes out of her mouth does not match. Another little adoptee from China, Shiloh joined the family two years before Braxton. Now seven, she's the most incorrigible kid I've ever met, with her round cheeks and square-cut bangs, and those mischievous dark eyes. She's adorable.

"How's it going, Shy?"

See, even her name's a contradiction.

"I'm pretty good. Life in the school yard is treating me well."

I press my lips together to stop from laughing. "Good to hear."

Roma places a glass of her homemade lemonade on the

counter in front of me and looks at her daughter. "You picked up your stuff yet?"

"All in good time, Moms." She raises her hand. "I'm conversing with the Samster right now."

Roma laughs and shakes her head. "Make sure it's put away before dinner is served."

"That can be arranged." Shiloh nods and turns towards the couch.

"And do *not* get Braxton to do it for you." Roma's voice is low with warning.

Shiloh's shoulders sag and she turns back to her mother with a dry glare. Roma just starts laughing again while Shiloh stomps off to pick up her stuff before dinner. I take a sip of my lemonade, then offer to help.

"Thanks, sweetie. That'd be great. Why don't you set the table?"

I head to the side cabinet and pull out the place mats.

"Set a place for yourself too!" Roma calls from the kitchen.

It's impossible to hide my grin as I slap an extra mat down before heading into the kitchen to grab the cutlery.

"So, how's skating going? Any new tricks up your

sleeve?" Roma tosses the salad, stealing out a square of feta cheese and nibbling while she works.

"Nothing too new. Just trying to work on nailing the stuff I already have."

"I can't tell you how incredibly cool you are."

"Me?" I scoff. "What about you?"

"What do I do that's cool?" She points a salad server at her chest.

"Uh, everything! You're like the coolest mom on this planet. You and Donnie are like a whole different breed of parent, believe me."

"I hope that's a good thing." Donnie appears on the other side of the kitchen, walking up to Roma and nuzzling her neck before stealing a cherry tomato out of the salad bowl.

I smile at him. "Trust me, it totally is."

"It's settled, we're keeping her." Donnie tips his head at me but is grinning at his wife. My insides warm with yearning when they say stuff like that.

If only.

"So, how's school treating you, Sams?"

"Good." I nod. "How's the security business?"

"Southern Idaho's never been safer." He winks at me.

"We just got in a bunch of new cameras and tech stuff, which I'm having fun playing with. Got some jobs in Brownridge tomorrow, so I'll get to test 'em out." He looks like a gleeful kid as he walks to the refrigerator.

Pulling out a root beer, he pops the cap and throws it into the living room. With a giggle, Braxton lifts his book and blocks the hit before scrambling off the couch and running at his father.

Donnie catches him with a growl, spinning him over his head before nestling him against his side. Braxton giggles again and rests his head on the big guy's shoulder.

My heart squeezes. I still remember when Braxton first arrived. He barely let anyone near him, but Donnie was the first to win him over. "So…" He takes a swig of his drink and saunters around the kitchen counter. "How's my favorite teenager?"

"Good." I laugh, walking back to the dining table and setting out the cutlery.

"Does Tyler know you're here?"

"I don't know if he's home yet."

"Yeah, I think he is." Donnie turns for the stairs. "Hey, Ty! There's a pretty girl here to see you."

My nose scrunches as I make a face. Donnie spins back in time to see the tail end of it. Wagging his finger at me, he mutters, "You know, one day I'm going to say that and you're actually going to believe me."

"Not likely," I mumble under my breath. I'm not a pretty girl. I never have been. I barely brush my hair in the morning. I mean, I'm clean and everything, but I'm not bothered about wearing the same clothes three days in a row. As long as they don't smell, I figure who cares.

"He's in the shower, Pop." Shiloh jumps off the last few steps and lands on the floor, right next to her upturned school bag. I hide my grin, kind of loving that she *still* hasn't put it away. She must have gotten distracted getting changed. She's now donned a pair of bright purple shorts with pink flamingos on them and a yellow tank top. Flicking her black hair over her shoulder, she sashays into the room and does a twirl before curtseying at her father's feet.

He gives her a tender smile and pats her head. "You know you're weird, right?"

"Proud to be." She beams at him.

"That's my girl." Scooping her up, he holds his two youngest against his sides and gives them a bear hug until they're both squealing.

I'm just setting out the last glass when Tyler appears at the bottom of the stairs. He pulls his T-shirt down over his torso and notices me standing by the table.

His smile is warm and familiar as he raises his chin at me. Running a hand through his wet hair, he musses it up before loping into the kitchen.

"How was track?" his mom asks him when he places a kiss on her cheek.

"Yeah, good." He turns to the fridge, pulling out a bottle of water and gulping it back. Braxton runs into the kitchen and wraps his arms around Tyler's muscular thigh, squealing as he hides behind it. Shiloh's skipping into the kitchen singing, "I'm gonna get you!"

And the squeals increase tenfold.

I wince at the piercing sound, but the rest of the Schumanns just laugh. Tyler picks up Braxton and extends his arms so his little brother is dangling in the air while Shiloh jumps around trying to touch his feet. He's laughing at Shiloh's attempts, dancing around the kitchen and nearly knocking a stack of plates off the counter. Donnie leaps forward to catch them while Roma taste-tests the dressing and then asks her husband if he's fed the dog yet.

As if reading her mind, Axel barks from the backyard, pressing his black nose against the glass. His tail is wagging like crazy as Donnie opens the back door. The dog bounds in, his claws clicking on the tiles as he dodges the kitchen traffic to come and greet me. I laugh, rubbing his head as he leans against my leg.

"Hey, buddy. How's it going?" He sniffs my waistband, letting out a satisfied snuffle as I rub behind his ears.

"Rome, where's the dog food? Did you move it?" Donnie's muffled question comes from the pantry, nearly drowned out by a new set of giggles from Shiloh. She's now sitting on Tyler's foot, trying to slow him down while he makes his way into the family room.

This place is so noisy and chaotic. It's the exact opposite of my house, and I absolutely love it. I feel more at home here than I do anywhere, and I can't even describe how badly I wish my name was Samantha Schumann.

5

SHE SAYS YES!

TYLER

I CAN'T TELL you how badly I wish my name was Mack Mahoney sometimes. The guy has it all. I mean, really, come on. He's the captain of the football team, one of the best players this school has ever seen. He could wear bright orange overalls to school and no doubt start a trend. He's not afraid of anything, and he's happy to skip prom because he can't take the girl he wants.

Even though Foxy Roxy Carmichael wants to go with him.

Seriously! Who does that?

I would give anything to go with that hot-bodied brunette. She's the epitome of cool. Dating her would put any guy in top position at Nelson High. But that's not the only reason I like her. I think she's awesome. She's pretty. She's smart. I know people think she's kind of bitchy, but I like her sharp tongue. She's got spunk, that's all.

Besides, I hang out with Sammy a lot. I can handle strong chicks.

Leaning against the wall, I watch Roxy strut into school while I wait for Sammy to lock up her bike. The thick chain clunks onto the pavement and she stands up, brushing her hands on the back of her jeans. I'm surprised they don't slip to the ground when she does that. Sammy likes two kinds of pants…either skinny, ripped-up jeans that look like they've been pilfered from a secondhand clothing bin or baggy skater-boy jeans that perch just on the edge of her hips. She tends to wear them with baggy T-shirts. She has an army of cotton shirts at her disposal, each with a different graphic or logo—skulls with roses for eyes, or *I kick ass, deal with it* type slogans. Today, she's in a short, black T-shirt with the Superman logo on the front. It's from Wal-Mart. Shiloh has the same one. I can't help grinning. My little sister would flip a switch if she knew she and Sammy had the same shirt. Shiloh adores the skater girl. She's even started asking for a board for her birthday.

Sammy flicks her long, fine hair out of her eyes and I

catch a glimpse of her skinny waist just before she ties a checkered shirt around it. The back flaps around her legs as she jumps over the bike stand and steps up beside me.

"You ready for that biology test today?" I ask her.

"No." She laughs. "I mean, kind of, I guess. I sort of looked over my book last night."

"Yeah, me too." I want to admit that I was distracted thinking about Roxy, but would Sammy find that weird?

I have the hots for her sister. It's kind of awkward.

We walk into the school and Sammy spins her cap around. I like it when she does that. You get a really clear view of her face. She's got this unique kind of beauty. I can't figure out if I like it because she's my friend or if she really *is* pretty. I've never thought of her that way before, so my brain stops the analysis before I can go too far. Having the hots for Sammy would be too weird.

I do love how tall and lean she is, though. Mack once said she reminded him of an elf from *The Lord of the Rings*. Totally! I can just imagine Sammy running around some forest with a bow and arrow, kicking ass and downing a bunch of orcs. She'd love it.

"Well, have a good day, man. I'll catch ya later." Sammy

bumps fists with me before we part ways and head for homeroom. I don't need to swing past my locker this morning, so I decide to head to class via Roxy's corridor. May as well grab one more glimpse of gorgeous before heading to class.

She sees me coming. I try to act like I didn't specifically walk down this hallway to see her. Using Colt as my perfect out, I head for his locker, but he doesn't see me and moves out of range before I get there. I'm not about to holler his name, so I just keep walking, trying to play it cool.

"Hey, Tyler." I practically jolt to a stop when Roxy says my name.

Pivoting toward her, I paste on what I hope is an unaffected smile and say, "How's it going?"

"Good." She tips her head with this sweet little grin and hands me a flyer.

It's bright pink and has the slogan: *Every girl can be a princess, but only one can be queen. Make the right choice and vote Roxy C for prom queen.*

"Nice." I bob my head, smiling at the sexy shot of her winking at the camera. Even photocopied onto pink paper, her face is beautiful.

My insides start acting like sherbet, fizzing and popping as she closes the gap between us. Her finger touches my shark tooth necklace as she bites the edge of her lip and looks up at me with those big blue eyes.

"So, we all know a prom queen really can't fly solo on her big night. I'm looking for a handsome prince to escort me to the ball." She giggles, then brushes her teeth over her glossy lip. "You know how you asked me to prom the other day, when Mack didn't want to go?"

"Yeah." I swallow.

"Did you mean it? Or were you just fooling around?"

"No, I meant it." I try not to sound too eager, but it's freaking hard. My voice nearly breaks over the words. I clear my throat and use the deepest voice I can. "I'd love to take you to prom. I can be your prince, Queen Roxy."

"Good." Her smile is so damn sexy right now. "Because I'd love to go with you."

A smile dominates my face. It's impossible to remain cool, suave, whatever the hell I should be. I'm taking Roxanne Carmichael to prom! How can I not smile? It's taking everything in me not to punch the air with a loud whoop!

"I'll, um, I'll get some tickets, then."

"Okay." She bobs her head. "I'll let you know the color of my dress once I've made my final decision, okay? I want to make sure we're matching. Who knows, if word spreads that Mack's not going, you might have a shot at prom king."

"You think so?"

"With me as your date? Highly likely." She giggles, then winks before spinning on her heel and walking away. I watch her hips sway and smile again when she glances over her shoulder and smirks at me.

The bell rings and it takes me a second to move. I can barely think straight. Roxy said yes! She said yes! And now I'm going to have the hottest date at prom.

It's gonna be the night of my freaking life!

6

DEVIL HORNS

SAMMY

"SAMANTHA," Mom chides as she steps into my room without knocking.

I really need to shut my door. If it's open even a crack she assumes free entry.

I look up from the *Empire* magazine I'm thumbing through and raise my eyebrows at her.

"What do you call this?" She points to the clothes on my floor.

Leaning over my bed, I peer down at the rumpled denim and quip, "I'm pretty sure those are jeans. And that over there looks like a cotton T-shirt."

Mom responds with an unimpressed glare. "Pick up

your clothes and put them in the hamper, and then take that hamper downstairs and put the clothes in the washing machine! Honestly, how can you be such a slob all the time? Your room is disgusting." She flicks her manicured finger at the clutter on my desk, then curls her lips at the posters on my ceiling. "When I agreed to let you decorate your own room, you said..." She shakes her head, starting up with the same old argument.

I groan. "Mom, would you get over it already! A deal's a deal!"

"Yes, exactly! And you're not keeping your end of the bargain."

"You said my room had to be clean. The word tidy was never mentioned."

"Oh, for goodness sake, Samantha!"

"The room is clean, Mom! I dust, I vacuum, it doesn't smell like stale underwear in here!"

She lets out a disgusted huff. "I never should have agreed to this. When I said yes, I thought you were going to do something similar to Roxanne."

"Really?" My forehead bunches with skepticism.

How stupid is this woman?

"Her room's so pretty, Samantha. I don't feel like I have

to close the door every time I walk past it. It's a girl's room, and whether you like it or not, you are actually a girl."

I don't have a response to the expression on her face right now. She's probably clueless as to how much it stings me. For a mother, you'd think she'd be better at hiding her disappointment in the fact that I'm not a lady like her and her precious Roxanne.

Getting off my bed, I snatch my jeans off the floor and reach for my shirt. "I'll put the wash on now," I grumble.

Mom sighs and turns out the door. "Make sure you put in the right amount of powder, and don't forget the softener. I know you don't care about these things, but I'd appreciate people in this town not thinking I can't look after my own children. I know you don't care, but appearances *do* matter. You need to be mindful of the impression you send out to the world every time you walk out the door dressed like a hobo."

She sniffs and leaves me to it. I clench my jaw and glare at the carpet, unable to move as I work through my anger. It's like a tornado in my chest—strong yet silent. I'll never let it show. Telling my mother the negative effect she sometimes has on me won't achieve anything. It'll just make her feel like she's failing at something else.

My family are experts at keeping the emotions on lock-down. Mom will never admit how much staying in a loveless marriage kills her, so she works overtime to present the perfect image to the world. It's her way of staying afloat...just like I'll never cry or get emo over the storm in my chest.

Grabbing my laundry hamper, I creep to the top of the stairs and check that Mom's out of view before scurrying to the laundry room and dumping the clothes in. I sprinkle some powder over my dirty clothes before adding a dash of softener. I quickly slam the lid shut before Mom catches me not doing it properly. The machine beeps when I switch it on, and I wait five seconds until I can hear the water running through the pipes before returning to my room.

Dad's in the den catching up on all the sports he missed while working. That seems to be his standard MO—work like a dog Monday to Friday, watch TV all weekend. It's actually a blessing, really; when the TV's on, they fight less.

"Roxanne, sweetheart." Mom knocks on Roxy's door. "Are you home?"

I reach the top of the stairs while Mom waits for a muffled reply from the pink room.

There's none.

She knocks again, wrapping her fingers around the door handle. "Roxanne?"

"Mom," Roxy whines. "It's Saturday, let me sleep."

"Okay, sweetie. I just wanted to let you know I got those magazines you asked for. When you're up, come down to the dining room so we can go over some prom dress ideas, okay?"

There's a short pause before Roxy chirps, "I'll be down after a shower."

Mom giggles, sounding like an excited tween. "See you soon. I'll make us some lattes."

I move out of the way so she can glide past me and down the stairs. She starts humming before she reaches the bottom, and I walk to my room before I have to bump into Roxy.

I close my door, but it doesn't block out the sound of muffled sports commentary from the den beneath my room or the sound of the shower starting up in the bathroom. I can't help wondering what's happening at the Schumann's house right now. I bet Tyler and Shiloh aren't getting lectured about the impression they send out to the world!

Flopping onto my bed, I stare up at the pictures on my ceiling. It took me an entire weekend, but I covered every inch of white with pictures of extreme sports people doing wicked stuff on their boards and bikes. Mom nearly had a fit when she saw what I'd done, but we'd made a deal—and after an all-out shout-fest with my father, she gave in and said she'd stick to it. But she did make me promise I'd keep my door shut every time I left the house.

Fine by me.

Rolling onto my side, I check the clock on my desk and groan. Saturdays with nothing to do are so freaking painful. Tyler wasn't free when I texted him this morning, and Darius and Will were doing weights. They offered to let me join, but I didn't feel like spotting today.

Sitting up, I eye my board and figure I may as well go skating; it's something to do, and it'll get me out of the house for a while. Dad's home until Tuesday, and until then it's like living inside a ticking time bomb. There have been no explosions since he got back from Portland, but it's only a matter of time. They've been keeping out of each other's way, but I don't want to be around when they collide.

Wriggling my feet into my worn Vans, I thump my heel down and manage to get them on without untying the laces. I'm just reaching for my board when my phone starts ringing.

A grin lights my lips before I even answer. "Hey, Ty. What's up?"

"I need your advice. Can you get down here?"

I frown at his question. "Where are you?"

"The suit shop down on Main. You know, the place that rents tuxes? I can't remember what it's called."

My nose wrinkles. "Why are you there?"

"Get down here and I'll tell you."

For some weird reason, my heart skips a beat because for a split second, I wonder if Tyler's about to ask me to prom. Like that would ever happen, but that flash of a thought, that one little entertainment, gets me all hyped up. I run downstairs and pull my bike out of the garage, cycling to Main Street with this goofy smile on my face.

As I'm locking up my bike, I try to talk myself out of the fantasy. But then logic steps up and argues so hard that I start thinking it's plausible. Tyler doesn't have a date. He probably wants to take a friend with him, someone he can enjoy the night with.

That's me!

We'll go together, dance like idiots, have a bunch of laughs, and it'll be the best night ever.

Funny, I wasn't even going to go to prom.

Running around the corner, I skip out of a lady's way, then duck past a couple on their cell phones. Stopping outside the suit shop door, I grip the handle and take a breath before walking in.

I find Tyler easily. He's outside the dressing rooms, checking himself out in the mirror. I've never seen him dressed up before and it makes me snicker.

He spins at the sound, his expression dropping with doubt. "I look like an idiot, don't I?"

"No! You look great!" I wave my hand up and down, pointing at the suit. "Totally stylin'. Your date's gonna love it."

"Oh man, I hope so." He smoothes down the jacket and swivels from side to side, looking uncharacteristically nervous.

What's he got to worry about? He's great with the ladies. Whoever he asks will say yes in a heartbeat.

The three-letter word is dancing around inside my mouth, desperate to break free. I press my lips together and then hope I sound casual when I mutter, "I know she will."

"Yeah?" Tyler's eyes light up. "Did she tell you already?"

My zinging insides screech like the police have just shown up to an underage rave. There's that horrified, frozen pause as my brain deals with the disappointment, and then chaos ensues as I try to figure out who he's really taking... and reality kicks my ass.

"W-what?" I stammer.

"Roxy. What did she say when she told you?"

"Roxy?" I breathe the word and then practically yell, "What!"

Tyler's goofy smile is starting to irritate me as a sick foreboding bubbles in my stomach.

"Roxy, your sister. I asked her to prom and she said yes. Can you believe it?"

I want to say no in a deep, metallic voice, but the truth is I *can* believe it.

"When did you ask her?" I'm speaking in a thin and raspy voice now.

Tyler's back to checking himself out in the mirror. "Tuesday, I think."

"And when did she say yes?"

"Yesterday."

I can *totally* believe it. That little...

My skin crawls as I recall the glint in my sister's eye when she noticed me checking out my best friend.

"It's cool, right?" Tyler leans into my view, snapping my eyes back into focus.

I somehow nod.

"So, she says she wants our outfits to match. Do you know what she's wearing?"

I shake my head.

"Okay." He tips his head. "Not really your thing. I get it." Spinning away from me, he dips into the changing room and pulls out another tux, holding it up so I can see it. "Do you think this one would be better?"

I shrug.

"Come on, Sammy. Help a guy out. Which do you think will look better on me?"

Both. You're freaking gorgeous. You look good in anything. You probably look even better in nothing!

I can't say any of that, of course. My tongue's still struggling to work past the truth that my sister is going to prom with *my* Ty! And if I know my sister like I think I do, there's probably a strong chance she will get to see him in nothing by the end of prom night.

A sick wave of dizziness crests over me as a red kind of rage blurs my vision.

This is so freaking unfair!

Roxy, the girl in our school who could get any guy she wants, goes after the only person I've ever liked.

"Hello. Earth to Sammy!" Tyler waves his hand in front of my face. "Are you okay?"

"Uh-huh." I clench my jaw and nod.

Tyler's face puckers with an uncertain frown. "It's okay that I'm taking your sister, right? I mean, I didn't think it would be a problem."

"It's not." I sniff, desperately trying to keep it together. "I like the one you're wearing." I point at his suit, my arms stiff and robotic.

"Cool." Tyler turns back to face the mirror, a large grin spreading across his face.

He looks so happy right now.

Closing my eyes, I turn away from him and pull out my phone, pretending to text someone.

"Hey, so do you want to go to the skate park after—"

"I gotta go," I cut him off and head for the door. "Congrats on the prom date, man."

"Thanks." He sounds kind of mystified as I walk away from him, but I really don't care. I'm too red and angry to do anything but storm out of the store.

Bursting into the sunlight, I pace away from the shop,

not realizing I'm going the wrong way until after I've been walking for a few minutes. Like hell I'm walking back past the shop; I'll just have to go the long way round.

I huff out a sharp breath and punch my fist in the air, nearly taking out a short girl beside me.

"Whoa!" She jumps out of the way, then giggles.

"Sorry," I mutter and keep walking.

"Hey, Sam. Are you okay?" It's not until she calls out to me that I recognize the voice.

Spinning on my heel, I face Tori with a sad smile. "Oh. Hey, Pix."

She brushes a curl off her cheek and walks up to me. "What's up? You look ready to kill something."

"Or someone," I mumble.

Tori's eyebrows rise as she stops in front of me. "Wanna talk about it?"

"No!"

"Okay." She nods, giving me another sweet smile that totally breaks me open.

"Tyler's taking Roxy to prom! Like she would ever notice him normally, but no, of course she sees me checking him out and then her little devil horns come out and she frickin' says yes to his invitation!"

Tori's stunned by my outburst.

Hell, so am I.

So much for keeping everything on lockdown!

Bunching my lips, I shake my head and get ready to storm off again.

"I always wondered how you felt about him." Tori's smile is gentle and endearing. "Falling for your best friend is a smart move. It's so much easier being with a guy you're friends with."

Her soft words make my eyes burn. I smash my teeth together and shake my head. "Only if he sees you as more than just a buddy."

Tori's face bunches with compassion. It's seriously not helping my burning eyeballs. I blink to ward off any kind of tears. I'm not the crying type, and like hell am I going to let my conniving sister be the cause of any kind of weep-fest.

Snapping my shoulders back, I stare down at Tori with flaring nostrils. "I'm not going to let her get away with this. She can't just steal the only guy I've ever liked right out from under me. It's not fair," I seethe. "I'm just going to have to shoot the gap."

Tori's eyebrows wrinkle. "Shoot the gap? You mean score with Tyler even though he's kind of with your sister now?"

"She's not even interested in him. She's just using him to irritate me. He's better than that." I spit out the words, then lose my breath as I whisper, "He's so much better than that."

I don't hear Tori's response. It's lost as I spin away from her and start running. A bunch of emotions are fueling me, giving me speed as I tear down the street. I don't know how I'm going to do it, but I will not just sit by and let the best guy I know be manipulated and played with by a girl who doesn't even know how to love him.

7

LEGENDARY

TYLER

OKAY, so Sammy's reaction in the store was a little off, but not enough to ruin my mood. I arrange to rent the suit on prom night and step out of the store with this stupid smile on my face. I can't help it. I'm taking Roxy to the prom! It's epic. It's legendary.

Legendary.

That word always makes me think of Sammy.

I hope she can make it to prom, as well. I wonder if I can score her a date somehow and then we could all go together. Rent a big limo or something. It'll be totally awesome. Maybe Will or Darius will want to take her. I would ask Finn, but he's kind of busy with Layla now.

Pursing my lips, I run through all the other guys on the

team, but none of them sit right. I can't imagine any of them strolling into the decorated gym with Sammy on their arm. It's way more her style to fly solo. A smile spreads my lips wide as I imagine her rolling in on her skateboard.

I laugh.

Oh, man, I so have to convince her to do that.

Slipping on my shades, I ruffle my hair and walk down the street, noticing how bright the sun is today, how crystal clear the blue skies are. My gaze travels across the expanse and then back to the street where I find Tori. She's waiting on the sidewalk, gripping her hippie bag strap and staring down the street.

A few months ago, I would have walked right past her, probably pretending I didn't notice she was there. Hey, she's short. I could get away with that excuse. But the truth is, I kind of like her now. She's seriously grown on me in spite of my efforts to keep her on the outskirts, so I slow my pace and amble up to the pixie girl.

"Hey, Pix. How's it going?"

She spins to face me, her smile a touch nervous. I don't know what that's about.

"You waiting for someone?"

"Yeah, Colt's meeting me here in a few minutes." She

points over her shoulder, then looks to the ground, tucking a curl behind her ear. The bracelets on her arm bunch together and I stare at the array of rings on her fingers. The topaz one on her forefinger is the biggest and always catches my eye. I also like the peace symbol on her thumb.

An awkward silence settles between us while I check out her hippy jewelry. Tori's not usually quiet. If anything, when she's nervous she gets a serious case of verbal diarrhea. I don't know what's going on right now and I don't want it to ruin my good mood, so I'm gonna bail.

I'm about to say goodbye and walk away when Tori's head shoots up and she points at the store behind me.

"So, suit shopping, huh? That's cool. You going to the prom? It's exciting, right? Who're you taking?"

The questions fire out of her mouth with a typical Tori swiftness. I snicker and rub a hand over my lips before answering.

"I'm taking Roxy."

"Cool." She smiles, her head bobbing like she already knows this.

My eyes narrow as I study her expression. She purses her lips and looks to the ground, her cheeks flaring with color. Glancing over her shoulder, I strain to see

Sam, but I don't recognize any of the people strolling along the sidewalk.

Did they bump into each other? What did Sammy say? I can't help being curious. Sammy was acting weird in the store.

"I'm happy for you that you've got a nice date." Tori smiles at me again, not meaning a word of what she's saying. It's no secret she doesn't like Roxy. I can tell by the strain of her smile that she's just trying to be nice.

I decide to go with it and pretend like she's genuine. "Yeah, I'm really stoked. Maybe we can all go together or something?"

Tori's face pulls into a skeptical frown. "I doubt Roxy would want me tagging along with your crowd."

"Yeah." My forehead wrinkles as I get a fast-forward of the night.

Will all my friends just end up going separately? It does seem kind of weird that Mack won't be there, and Colt and Tori probably won't be hanging with us because of the rift between the two girls. At least Finn and Layla will be cool.

"You, uh... You sure you want to go with Roxy?"

Tori's quiet question makes my head snap around. I face her with a slightly incredulous look, my voice pitching high. "Of course! Why wouldn't I? She's

Roxy freaking Carmichael. I'll have the hottest date there. Hey, I might even have a shot at prom king, right?"

"Yeah." Tori shrugs. "But… I mean, I just…" Her lips purse again and she starts fidgeting with one of the tassels hanging off the bottom of her bag.

"You just what?" I snap. "You don't think I'm prom king material?"

"No! You absolutely are." She clears her throat. "It's just… I was talking about Rox…" She plays with her topaz ring, pulling it back and forth over her knuckle. "Being the hottest doesn't make her the best, you know? I mean…" She shakes her head and brushes the air with her hand. "Doesn't matter."

I open my mouth to try and find out what the hell she's not saying, but I'm shut up by Colt. He's walking up to us with a fiery look in his eyes, warning me off with his usual set of daggers. I roll my eyes and raise my hands.

"Chill, man. We were just chatting."

"Were you being nice?" he asks sharply, wrapping his arm around Tori's shoulders.

"Yeah, he was." Tori smiles up at him. "We were just talking about prom."

Colt's face relaxes into an easy smile. "Oh, cool."

I fire him one more dry glare for being so overprotective. His response is a sheepish grin.

I shake my head and move on. "I'm taking Roxy."

Colt blinks a couple of times and then chokes out, "Really?"

"Don't sound so surprised, you big douche." I swing forward with a light punch.

He steps into it, blocking Tori and laughing as I catch his arm. "Nice going, man. You guys will look great together."

"Yes, we will." I nod, sounding all superior as I imagine walking into the decorated space with that hottie on my arm. People are going to look. Sure, they might be a little surprised, but I'm going to prove them all wrong. It's out of the shadows for me. I'm going to be a freaking supernova that night.

Colt snickers at my expression and then says goodbye. I lift my chin. "See you guys later."

Tori waves her fingers at me, then giggles as Colt whispers something in her ear before pressing his lips against her neck. She wraps her arm around his waist and looks up so they can kiss properly. And I'm snatched by a sudden chill.

Those two look so comfortable and easy together. I can't imagine Roxy making me feel that calm and secure. If anything, prom's going to make her realize the truth about me—that I'm no sex-god...that I'm actually full of shit. It's not enough for me to pull out of this, but it's enough to make me nervous.

What if she wants more after the prom? Shit, she probably will, and then I'm done for. My big mouth is going to come back and bite me in the ass.

This prom thing is a bigger risk than I thought. I mean I'm still going to do it, but...

Running a hand through my hair, I scratch the back of my head. I can't help but think that it'd be so much easier to take the other Carmichael sister. And what the hell am I doing asking a girl who's way out of my league?

8

TAKING SIDES

SAMMY

THROWING my bike on the front lawn, I ignore Mom's rule to always park it in the garage and storm through the house, slamming the door with as much force as I can. The sound blasts through the house, alerting everyone to my mood. I don't care. I'm pissed, and yelling at someone might help me unleash some of this steam.

"Samantha? What is going on?"

I ignore Mom's question and turn away from her, spotting my sister at the dining room table. She's surrounded by her girly fashion magazines, little sticky notes poking out the top like bookmarks. The laptop on the table is open, a Pinterest page full of prom dresses on the screen. She looks from the screen back down to her magazine, pretending not to notice my presence.

As if. That triumphant little smirk on her face is killing me!

Slapping my hand over the thin, glossy pages, I slide the book out of her hands and glare down at her.

"Hey, sis. How was your morning?" I hate her chipper tone, that knowing little glint in her eyes.

"Why? You don't even like him." Great, my voice sounds broken already.

"I never said that." She shrugs, reaching past me to retrieve her magazine. I snatch it out of her hand, the pages ripping before I throw it on the floor.

Her light amusement is scarred by a threatening look that does nothing to frighten me.

"You should have said no!"

"Why, because he's going to ask you?" She shoots out of her chair. "Get real, Sammy. He treats you like one of the guys. He doesn't even think of you that way. He wants to take a real girl to the prom, and I'm happy to go with him. I didn't realize how hot he was. You helped me notice that the other day." She gives me a grateful smile.

I want to slap her face right now!

"Besides, he's funny. I like him. In fact, the more time I spend with him, the more I realize what a great guy he is."

"You're spending time with him? When? You've never even liked him before."

Roxy gives me her *oh, you're so bothersome* sigh and looks down at her nails. "When have I ever said that?"

"Oh, please, you've never given him the time of day! You probably wouldn't have even noticed him if you hadn't seen me checking him out!"

"Whatever." She flicks her hand in the air. "You think you see everything with your beady little eyes, but you really don't. Go back to your skate ramp. It's where you belong, and it's the only place you're ever going to shine."

A puff of air shoots out of my nose as I go to fist her collar.

"Samantha!" Mom's sharp warning stops me. "Don't even think about it. You treat your sister with respect."

I scoff. "Like she's treating me?"

"Okay." Mom slowly cuts her hands through the air as if the smooth movement will calm everything down.

"I'm sure we can sit down and talk through this like ladies."

"Yeah, right! Ladies. Sure. That's gonna work. Roxy doesn't care. She's made up her mind and she's going to get exactly what she wants. Just like she always does!"

"Now, Samantha, let's not go through this again. Roxanne does not get special treatment in this family."

I roll my eyes and look to the ceiling. I'm so sick of this conversation. Is everyone really so blind?

"Sorry about the commotion, Mom." Roxy's voice is irritatingly calm and sugary. "Sam's a little disappointed because this guy has asked me to the prom and she doesn't think I'm good enough for him."

"Samantha," Mom scolds. "Why would you say that?"

"I didn't!" I throw my arms wide and glare at Roxy. "Although, it *is* the truth. You're not good enough for him. He deserves to go with someone who actually cares about who he is."

"Like you?" Roxy's expression is so pitiful I want to smash my fist right into that stupid little mouth of hers. "I thought we'd already established this. You aren't even female in our school, okay? Guys don't see you that way, ergo they're not going to ask you to prom. Don't be jealous of me because you dress and act like a boy all the time."

"Well, we can solve this." Mom chirps with a bright smile. "Roxanne, why don't you give your sister a makeover?" She steps up to me, collecting up my long strands of loose hair and running her fingers through them. "You could look so pretty."

I brush her hand off me, trying to convey how much that hurts without actually saying anything.

When am I going to be good enough as is?

"Bianca, leave her alone." Dad steps into the room. "She looks fine just the way she is." As grateful as I am for his sentiments, I really don't want him getting involved in this one.

My muscles ping tight as he stands beside me, creating a standoff between the two factions of our house. I can see the invisible line drawn on the floor between us. Roxy and Mom versus Dad and me. It's always the same...and I always hate it.

"Hayden, please. Let me deal with the girls. We don't need your input on this one." Mom's bright tone is so forced, her smile tight enough to break her face.

"Well, you're getting it. Sam doesn't need to improve her looks and if anything, Roxy should be apologizing for the way she just spoke to her sister!"

"It's okay, Dad." I brush the air, hoping to diffuse the mounting tension.

"No, it's not okay. Roxanne." Dad tips his head at me.

"Like hell!" she responds, crossing her arms. "She storms in here, rips up my magazine, goes off on me because she's jealous. I don't think I should have to apologize for anything. It's not my fault a perfectly nice guy asked me to prom. The least she could do is be happy for me."

I clench my jaw while Roxy blinks her eyes, putting on her innocent *feel sorry for me* face.

"I agree." Mom looks between me and Dad. "Samantha, this is your sister's last prom. I don't think it's fair to ruin it. Next year you can have your big night, but it's Roxy's turn." Mom leans in and puts her arm around my sister.

"It's always Roxy's turn," I grumble.

"You shouldn't be showing favoritism, Bianca." Dad frowns. "Just because Sammy's a little different doesn't mean you need to treat her that way. You've always disapproved of the fact that she just wants to be herself. It makes me feel like I can't leave you alone with the girls if you're going to treat one like a queen and the other like a dog."

I roll my eyes. Here we go.

"Leave them alone with me? Is that what you just said?" Mom's eyes burn bright as she glares at Dad. "Are you accusing me of being a bad parent? Because if we're pointing fingers, I've got a pretty long list for you!"

Dad steps in front of me, his fat finger aiming at Mom's face as they get into it.

"Don't start with me. I'm working my ass off for this family, trying to provide you girls with everything you need. Do you have any idea how much Roxy's gown is costing? Yeah, I heard you talkin', and I'm not shelling out that much money for a stupid dress!"

"It's her last prom! Be reasonable. She deserves to look her best."

"Her best? It's a frickin' dress, Bianca! And she'll probably only end up wearing it for one night."

"Oh, you know nothing! Go back to your sport shows and let me run this house!"

"So, I'm just the finance department then, am I? I have no say in what goes on under this roof?"

"You're never here to have a say!"

"You wanted me to take this job!"

I cringe at Dad's thundering tone, easing out from behind him and making my way to the stairs.

"Nice going, idiot," Roxy mutters as I follow her up the stairs.

She's right. I should have known better than to slam into the house and go off on Roxy. I should have known it would only lead to the perfect excuse for my parents to start yelling at each other. The old arguments rear their ugly heads so quickly.

Easing into my room, I gently shut the door behind me and lean against the wood. I'd do anything to skate to Tyler's place right now and spend the rest of the day hanging out with him and his amazing family.

But I can't.

Tyler's taking my sister to prom, and being around him is just going to be weird now. I don't know what I'm gonna do.

Sliding to the floor, I stretch my legs out in front of me and resist the urge to cry. My stupid sister's not getting one of my tears. None of them are.

The only thing I can really do is fight back and prove to the *perfect* Roxanne that she's not the only Carmichael who can catch a guy's eye. I gaze down at my body, a doubtful frown flickering over my expression. Slapping the floor, I let out a little huff and jump up, walking to my dresser and pulling out every item of clothing I have.

"I can do this," I keep muttering as I fling the clothes over my shoulder.

Too bad I don't quite believe what I'm saying.

9

SAMMY'S GOT BOOBS

TYLER

AS AWESOME AS my weekend started, it kind of ended on a downer. Sammy didn't want to go skating with me on Sunday, which is way weird. That chick never passes up the chance to get on her board, but she said she was busy. I was tempted to text Roxy and see what she was doing, but I doubted she'd want to watch me and the guys skate all afternoon, so I just hung out with Darius and Will. It's safe to say that hanging out with those idiots, minus Sammy, is only half as cool, and I came home in a slightly foul mood.

I ended up taking Axel for a run and then played *Just Dance* with Shiloh, which perked me up a little, but not enough to chill the niggle inside me.

I don't like things being difficult with Sammy and for

some weird reason, they kind of are. Maybe she's annoyed I'm taking Roxy to prom. I don't know why she would be, and because we're not about the deep and meaningfuls, I won't bring it up when I see her.

Instead, I'm going to come back to our little paparazzo investigation. Talking about something neutral will totally get us back on track.

Walking down the hall to her locker, I snicker when I spot a few cheerleaders strutting past in bright pink shirts. *Roxy's my queen! Make her yours too!* is written on the front in swirly writing. My eyes start rolling before I can stop them. As much as I love her spunk and determination, I can't help wondering if Roxy's going a little OTT with the whole prom queen campaign. Of course she's going to get voted for queen.

A lump forms in my throat as I wonder if I'll be crowned king. That would be epic. Hopefully, all of Roxy's campaigning will rub off on me like osmosis or something, because the guys will never let me live it down if I turn into some kind of politician wooing the student body for votes.

Turning the corner, I spot Sammy at her locker, her long hair swept over her shoulder, and am struck by how different she is to Roxy. Never in a million years would Sammy try to get in people's faces and sell how awesome she is. As much as I love Roxy's tenacity, I also really love Sammy's way too. She has this understated cool kind of vibe—*I'm me. You don't like it? You can stick it.*

I snicker. Yeah, that would totally be Sammy's slogan.

"Hey, Skater Girl." I lean against the locker beside hers and smile at a group of girls walking past us.

The hallways are busy with morning traffic and I need to keep this brief before the bell rings. Sammy doesn't look at me. Her eyes are trained on the inside of her locker and her jaw's clenched. She looks nervous…or maybe pissed?

Shit, I hate this.

Clearing my throat, I run a hand through my hair and launch straight into my plan, hoping like hell it will clear the air between us. "So, I was thinking about the photo thing last night, and I was wondering if we should get in with the photography club or something."

Her head snaps to face me, her blue eyes kind of piercing. I've always liked her eyes. The blue hoodie she's wearing totally makes them pop.

"Dude, I am not joining that. I don't do anything with the words 'club' or 'committee' in them."

I grin. Yes, we're back on track.

"I'm not saying join." I lightly slap her arm with the back of my fingers. "I was just wondering if you could pretend to show interest or something and then subtly get people talking. Those photos were pretty crystal clear."

She shrugs, shoving a textbook into her locker before zipping up her bag. "You can take clear shots on a phone."

"Come on, Sammy." I nudge her shoulder with my fist. "I need you to think this idea is really cool."

Slapping her locker closed, she turns to me with a smirk. I match her expression until she starts to laugh. "Okay, fine, it could work." She hitches her bag onto her shoulder. "Roxy got some expensive camera Mom bought her for Christmas. I'll see if I can borrow it and play dumb for a couple of days. Maybe ask one of them to show me how to get all technical with the thing and subtly see if I can't get some legit info at the same time."

"Thank you." I nod.

Her right eyebrow arches. "What are you gonna do?"

I grin. "I'm going to get friendly with some of the year-book crew. Ricco's on there, plus I think Michelle is too. I'll make up some excuse about needing goods on Roxy for the prom and see if she remembers anything from that party."

Sammy dips her chin, then her head starts bobbing.

"Why don't you just ask Roxy? We both know she was there."

I purse my lips, not loving the fact she's been brought into the conversation. I don't want Sammy to get all clammed up again. I shrug and look to the floor. "I just don't want to drag her into this, you know?"

Sammy's eyes are drilling into me. I can feel it. This is going to get awkward way fast if I don't change the subject. I kind of hate that the sisters aren't best friends. It'd make things so much easier if they were.

I'll keep my eyes down until Sammy lets up. I'm pretty sure she'll back off soon. I know, I'll watch her feet. As soon as she steps back, I'll know I'm in the clear.

The sound of a zipper draws my eyes back up.

Sammy slips the hoodie off her shoulders, catching her bag before it thumps to the floor. She starts tying her sweatshirt around her waist, but I'm barely noticing because all I can see right now is boobs.

Holy crap!

Sammy's got boobs!

My mouth goes dry as I take in Sammy's tight little tank. It's one of those ones that dips low at the front and has two little buttons. The top one's undone.

It's undone!

And I can see the smooth curve of her breasts tucked into a white cotton bra. I mean, I can't really see the bra, just the very edge of it. I've never seen her in this top before.

Did she steal it off Roxy?

Damn. She's...pretty...

Sexy.

That can't be right.

It's Sammy I'm looking at here.

My eyes track down her body, cresting her slender waist, admiring the way her ripped-up skinny jeans hug her hips. I've never noticed that before. I've always just thought of her as skinny, but those legs have got some shape to them. I track the contour of her calf muscles, then pop back up to her chest. I can't stop gaping at her.

And what's with the fever spiking through me? My brain's trying to compute the idea that my best friend is making me feel something I shouldn't.

"What are you wearing?" I blurt.

Her eyes bulge for a second but then she recovers and glares at me. "They're called clothes, dumb ass."

"Where'd you get that top?" I choke. "I mean, I..." Clearing my throat, I point to the star-spangled banner skull on the front of her shirt and mumble, "Like the skull."

"Shut up." She shoves my shoulder.

I can't help looking down at her boobs again. They're so… I like the shape of them. They're a nice size, like they would fit perfectly into the palms of my hands.

Shit! Did I just think that?

This is insane!

I shut my eyes and look away from her, scratching the back of my head as I try not to think about the rest of her body too. She's obviously strong, but in this really sexy, athletic way. I can't help wondering what she'd look like in a skimpy dress…or a bikini.

"Stop being a dick." She smacks my arm with the back of her hand just as the bell rings.

I rub my arm and laugh, trying to hide the effect that show of skin is having on me. She rolls her eyes and heads off, unwrapping the sweatshirt from around her waist and pulling it back on. Good idea. I don't like the idea of other guys checking her out.

I stop short.

Why?

Why don't I like that?

"Oh, just stop thinking, you idiot," I mutter, clutching my bag and stalking off to class.

My mind completely ignores me, of course, and I'm soon scrambling to remember seeing Sammy in a bathing suit. But all I can picture her in is board shorts and a muscle tee as we jump off the rocks into the lake. Over the height of summer, I'm usually hanging out with my older sister and the rest of my family in Myrtle Beach.

Maybe I'll invite Sammy to join us this summer.

A grin spreads across my face as I picture Skater Girl running into the surf with me...in a string bikini. My mind does this little hiccupping explosion and I let out a nervous, slightly confused laugh as I head to class.

10

NO COMPETITION

SAMMY

I WALK INTO THE LIBRARY, tugging the hem of my baggy T-shirt as I go. I swear I am never wearing low-cut tank tops again. I don't even know why I put it on. My argument with Roxy and Mom's suggestion of a makeover really threw me. I don't know what came over me on Monday, but I grabbed the shirt I'd found buried in the back of my drawer and like a total idiot, put it on.

Insane.

The look on Tyler's face when he asked what I was wearing... so freaking humiliating. After sweltering through first period with my hoodie zipped up to my neck, I ditched school and went home to change, then spent the rest of the day at the skate park. One good thing about not being part of a clique is that no one ever bothers asking where you are.

On Tuesday, I got pulled up by my homeroom teacher for skipping out and have had detention every day after school this week. I really don't care; it saves me having to hang out with Tyler too much. I'm not sure I'll ever be able to look him in the eye again...even though I stupidly agreed to meet him in the library so we can work on our world history assignments together.

Shoving my hands in my pocket, I shuffle past the library desk and head to the study tables. I'm kind of behind on my school work, and after my grilling and week of detention I really need to up my game if I have any hope of the C+ average I'm aiming for. At least with Tyler there I'll be more motivated to stare at the books in front of me.

I walk around the cozy reading area and pop into the main part of the library to find Tori and Layla sitting at one of the tables together. Roxy's there too, but I'm trying to ignore that part. Layla has a large binder open in front of her, along with a laptop. Tori is pointing between the two with this teacher kind of look on her face.

And Roxy is, of course, throwing them disgruntled glares every time she looks up from her notepad.

My smile grows pretty big as I watch. I kind of like that Tori and Layla have formed this unlikely friendship.

Roxy can stick it.

I let out a derisive snort and walk over to the table.

Dumping my bag down next to their little tutoring session, I take a seat and exchange an icy scowl with my sister.

"What are you doing in a library?" She smirks at me.

I smirk right back. "I could ask you the same thing. Must be uncomfortable using that brain of yours for something other than the color pink and dress designs."

Her eyebrows dip into a V but then she shrugs and grins at me. "Well, for those of us who have dates to prom, we need to think about those things...unlike you...who has no one."

I turn away from her derisive comments and catch Tori watching the exchange. Her eyes are kind of wide and full of sympathy. I shake my head at her. I know she's not saying anything, but I really want her to shut up already. Like Roxy needs to know how much she's riling me. I want her to think I'm over it...like I don't give a shit that she and my Ty are going to prom together and will probably make out and have sex and...

Okay, this is killing me.

Forcing a smile, I decide to throw one more little punch before getting on with my work. "Prom's one night of your life, Roxy. Who gives a shit?"

Her eyebrows pop high, and she blinks at me like I'm a crazy person. "Uh, normal people with actual lives, who don't walk around this school by themselves all the time like some lonesome loser."

"I'm not by myself all the time," I snap.

"Oh, really?"

"Yeah." I nod. "In fact, Tyler's meeting me here any minute so we can work on our World War II assignments together." I sit back with a triumphant smile, crossing my arms and not even caring if I look like an arrogant prick right now.

Two points for Sammy.

Roxy's right eyebrow arches—a pathetic counterattack, if you ask me. Pulling her stupid-ass duck face, she caps her pen and rises from the table.

"Where are you going?" I frown. It's so unlike her to retreat.

"To find the book I need to help me study. That's what a library's for, right?" I wish her scathing looks weren't so similar to Mom's. I hate how much they sting. "Besides, I need something to keep me occupied while you little people work together on your assignments."

She struts away from the table and I can't resist flipping her the bird.

Layla snickers and then bites her lips together, cutting off the sound.

"Sorry," she mumbles, but she can't help smiling. "I shouldn't laugh, but I love the way you don't put up with any of Roxy's shit. You're really good at it."

"I should be," I mutter. "It's a full-time job."

Layla grins again, her brown eyes catching me off guard when her expression changes. "Hey, is there something going on with you and Tyler?"

I slump forward with a frown. "No, and in case you think I'm lying…I don't want to talk about it."

Pulling the notepad out of my bag, I slap it down on the table. Layla and Tori exchange some look I don't want to try to decipher. I put the pen in my mouth and rip off the cap, spitting it across the table. It bounces and clicks before rolling onto the floor. Spinning the pen in my fingers, I'm unable to think past my disgruntled anger.

Where the hell is Tyler?

I wish he'd hurry up already. Study hall finishes in like half an hour.

"So, uh, Layla's working on her world history assignment, too." Tori grins, way too obviously trying to break the tension.

I cut her some slack and force a smile. "I hate that thing."

"I know, right?" Layla flicks her hands in the air. "Still can't believe we got lumped with an assignment like this so close to the end of the year."

"At least it's the last one." Tori smiles.

I rest my elbows on the table. "I just want this year to be over already."

"Tell me about it," Layla murmurs, tapping her pen on the notepad in front of her.

Tori and I share a knowing look. She probably thinks I'm referring to the lake fight because she doesn't know that I know about the photos. Man, I wonder how bad they really are. I'd love to see one, just to satisfy my curiosity. The fact Tyler's so riled over them says a lot.

I must get Roxy's camera and head over to the photography club. I've been so focused on avoiding Tyler this week that I kind of forgot about my mission.

"So, um…" I clear my throat, hoping neither of the

girls are mind readers. "What are you doing your assignment on?"

"Tori did hers on the French resistance last year. I kind of like that idea, so I'm thinking I'll do the same." Her large eyes flick to Tori with a pleading look. "Unless she wants to give me hers and I could just like…copy it?"

Tori tips her head. "I actually meant it when I said no the first time. You'll get no satisfaction out of cheating."

"Are you sure about that?" Layla bites the edge of her lip. "Because the idea of not doing the assignment sounds pretty satisfying to me."

Tori giggles, her wild curls hitting the table as she leans forward. "I know you want to get out of this but seriously, if you put in the effort you'll be so proud of yourself. *I'll* be proud of you!"

I snort. "You're such a teacher."

She grins. "Thank you. I'm liking that idea more and more."

"Well, you'll make a good one."

"That's what Colt says." Her blush is vibrant.

Layla looks at me and winks. Tori is so loved-up, it's

almost comical. I'm really happy for her. So glad Colt opened his eyes and saw the light.

"So, what are you doing yours on, Skater Girl?"

"Absolutely no idea." I shrug. "I kind of haven't even read the assignment brief yet."

"Oh my gosh! Heart palpitations!" Tori taps her chest. "You haven't even started? I would be freaking out right now."

"It'll be fine." I brush my hand through the air. "I'll just pull an all-nighter. I'm not worried about it."

Tori cringes. "I so could not do that."

I snicker. "It's just an assignment, Pix. Nothing worth twisting my panties over."

Layla laughs and I can't help wondering if she's skeptical that I wear panties. She probably thinks I'm sporting tighty-whities under my cargo pants.

Shrinking down in my seat, I look away from the stunning brunette in her fitted blouse and tight little mini skirt. I bet no one stares at her boobs like a couple of aliens just popped out of her chest. I had no idea mine were so bad until Tyler made me realize they shouldn't be on public display.

Like the skull. He'd practically choked out the words while his eyes bulged at my chest.

Ugh. Wish I'd never put that damn tank top on.

"Okay, so French resistance." Tori taps the table. "Layla, start researching those questions we came up with together. Sammy, head down the 900 aisle and start looking for books on World War II. Let's see if we can't find a war story that sparks your interest."

I make a face but she flicks her thumb over her shoulder and gets me moving. With a huff, I rise from my chair and head for what I assume is the history section.

"900 aisle," I chuckle under my breath. "Can't believe she knows that by heart. What a nerd."

I walk slowly, happy to use up the time while I wait for Tyler's slow ass.

School's never really been my thing. I mean, I'll graduate and everything, but my real passion is skating and you don't need a degree to do that…and you definitely don't need to know anything about the Second World War.

With a sigh, I swing into the non-fiction section and am about to start scanning the Dewey decimal number tags when a soft groan catches my attention. It's followed by a heavy puffing sound that makes me grimace.

Gross. Why do people always make out back here?

Making a gagging face, I wander down the parallel aisle

searching for the 900s, but it's kind of hard to concentrate with the heavy make-out noises as my soundtrack.

Seriously! A little class, people. Come on.

I run my finger along the books, trying to ignore what's going on so close by. I'm embarrassed to say that I'm tempted to sneak a peek. I don't know why my curiosity works this way. It's kind of like the cheerleading thing. I can't help watching car wrecks.

My nose twitches as I try to resist the temptation, but I soon can't help myself. I snicker as I imagine telling Tyler about it later. He'll expect nothing less than a full report back…if I can find the guts to talk to him that way again.

Easing around the corner, I snatch a quick look down the aisle and feel my heart stutter and then clunk to a stop. The air in my lungs evaporates and I can't move for a second.

Tyler.

Roxy.

Tongues.

Bodies.

Hands.

Shit! His hand is resting on her waist right now, lightly squeezing it while she buries her fingers in his hair.

Roxy's tongue darts out of her mouth, curling around Tyler's. She lets out this little mewling sound and he moans against her lips.

I can see lipstick smears on his neck.

My blood feels like oil, slick and toxic as it runs through my body. Pounding head syndrome kicks in, and all I can do is gape at *my* Ty making out with a person I wish I wasn't related to.

A million points for Roxy.

She knows.

She knows exactly what she's doing.

I mean, doesn't she?

My jaw works to the side as my eyes start to burn again. Squeezing them shut, I spin away from the harrowing scene. Rubbing the sting with my thumb and forefinger, I work to pull my face into one of placid indifference. By the time I reach the table, I think I've got the bored look nailed.

"You find anything?" Tori looks at me, hopeful and expectant.

"Nothing worth looking at," I mutter. Snatching the bag off the chair, I barely offer them a goodbye as I storm out of the library, trying to outrun the scene I've just witnessed…and the idea that maybe Roxy isn't just playing.

She looked pretty into that kiss. If she didn't like Tyler a little, she wouldn't be letting him shove his tongue down her throat.

She said I didn't know everything.

Maybe she *is* into Tyler. Maybe she's not just using him.

Somehow that seems so much worse. Because if Roxy and I are competing for the same guy… I'm gonna lose.

11

THE OPPOSITE OF ROXY

TYLER

I CAN'T GET Roxy out of my head as I jog along the footpath. Axel's practically taking me for a run, his long legs eating up the ground beneath us. I barely notice. I'm still back in that secluded corner of the library. When Roxy saw me walk in, she took my hand with this sexy little smile on her face and pulled me over there. Her tongue was in my mouth before I could even say hello, and I just went with it. What guy wouldn't! It was freaking hot, her luscious curves pressed against me as she ran her fingers through my hair. It was like being caught in an electrical storm. I kind of didn't know what to do with myself.

I mean I did, but...

Thing is, I've made out with girls before, but something always stops me from going too far.

It's this little concept of big mouth plus no experience makes me look like a total fraud. So rather than working it out and becoming the stud I claim to be, I tend to get the girl to a total state of fluster (you know, craving more) and then back off and whisper something like, "Until next time, gorgeous."

It's worked for me in the past.

The problem with this time around is that I wasn't playing tonsil hockey with some sweet little freshman. I was getting hot and heavy with an experienced chick. I could tell she knew exactly what she was doing as she rubbed her body against mine.

She wanted more, and I was somehow supposed to give it to her.

I kind of don't know what to do. I thought I was lucky just to be taking Roxy to prom. I never expected her to start treating me like a boyfriend or something, but she totally has. She's started sitting with me at lunch, winking at me as we pass in the corridor...then making out with me in the library.

It's awesome. I'm not complaining or anything, but these silent expectations are being laid down every time she flirts with me. I'm worried it's all going to culminate at prom and I'll end up making a raving fool of myself.

And you don't want to act like a fool around Roxy Carmichael.

Axel barks and surges forward, nearly wrenching my arm out of its socket.

"Hey!" I yell, having to let go of the lead so he can bound into the skate park.

A deep chuckle that's so familiar and comforting reaches me, and I instantly feel myself relax. Walking up the small slope, I stop by the ramp and enjoy watching Sammy get licked to death by my dog.

"Nice to see you too." She laughs, squeezing her eyes shut as Axel's big tongue slobbers all over her face. "Okay, okay." She rubs behind his ears and stands tall.

I amble over, relieved when she grins at me. Things have been kind of weird this week. Sammy hasn't been her normal self. She even bailed on me at the library, which she's never done before. I haven't asked her why yet. We've barely spoken at school. It's like she's been avoiding me or something.

So, to see her standing there smiling is kinda nice.

I can't help skimming her body while she's not looking. She's back to her baggy T-shirts and cargo pants today. It's a relief…and a disappointment.

Weird how it's both. I should be more relieved than anything—my old Sammy is back. So why am I picturing that tank top all over again, imagining what kind of bra she has on under the black Vans T-shirt she's wearing right now?

Seriously, Ty?

Stop thinking about Sammy's underwear!

I clear my throat and scramble for a topic change, grateful Sammy can't read minds.

"I swear this dog loves *you* more than me." I scratch Axel's hind legs, his long tail thumping me.

"Well, he's intelligent." Sammy grins at the Great Dane. "Aren't you, boy?"

Axel's tail goes crazy, whacking against my sweaty leg while Sammy makes little kissing noises. He jumps up, resting his hands on her shoulders and giving her another lick.

"Hey, get down." I use my firm voice, gently tugging his lead.

He plops back down and settles at Sammy's feet, leaning against her as he stretches out on the grass.

She gazes down at him with this wistful kind of longing on her face. She's always wanted a dog, but her mom's got this thing about pets messing up the house. I'm often struck by how much Sammy doesn't fit in her home. I wish she'd been born into mine. It's always so easy having her around. It's like she belongs there.

Thank God I have my parents and not hers.

Perching my butt on the picnic table, I cross my arms and look at her.

"I feel like I haven't seen you much this week. Want to come over for dinner tonight?"

"Yeah, maybe." Her left shoulder hitches. "You're not busy?"

I frown. "Busy? What do you mean?"

"You know, with my sister." Her left eyebrow arches, making her narrow face look even longer.

The way she's looking at me right now has a warning alarm sounding in the back of my brain. "Why are you looking at me like that?"

She smirks. "I saw you guys making out yesterday. You know, when you were supposed to be studying with me?"

I swallow and scratch my neck. "I thought you bailed."

"Yeah, well, when I saw you were a little tongue-tied, I figured it wasn't gonna happen, so I left."

"Shit. Sorry, Sammy. I didn't know you were in the library."

"I'm sure you weren't aware of a lot of things." Her eyes bulge. "That make-out session looked pretty intense…and disgusting." She sticks her tongue out.

I snicker and shake my head, my cheeks heating to molten-lava temperature.

"Uh…" I run a hand through my hair and scratch the back of my neck. "I got nothing."

"You got somethin' going on."

Her pointed look makes my face pucker with a frown. "Is it weird? You know, being your sister and everything."

"No." She shrugs. "I mean, yeah. It is."

I laugh as her head bobs like crazy, but the sound is cut short as this horrible thought hits me.

"Hey, it's not enough to stop us being friends though, right?" I sound more worried than I mean to. But come on, losing Sammy would suck.

Her blue eyes hit me then, saying something I don't quite understand. I've never seen such an intense look from her before…like she's going to cry or something.

"Are you okay?" I stand up from the table, ready to hug her…or bolt from the scene.

I don't know. I'm not good with feelings and shit.

"I'm friends with you, Tyler. Of course I'm not okay." Her dry quip eases my nerves, and I relax again when she crouches down and starts petting Axel. His tail starts thumping the second she touches him.

I watch the sweet exchange, comforted by Sam's derogatory comment. I'm glad Roxy's not going to come between us. I feel like I can't back out of the prom thing now, even though I'm a little worried about what might follow. Chewing the edge of my lip, I stare at the ground, consumed by those damn expectations.

"Did you forget to eat lunch today, or are you just wearing a really tasty lip gloss?" Sammy smirks.

I glance at her raised eyebrow and can't help a laugh. Walking over to her, I crouch down to run my hands down Axel's long torso.

"It's your sister. I never *ever* thought she'd notice me."

Sammy's nose twitches but she keeps her eyes focused on the top of Axel's head...giving me nothing. This is probably weird for her, but I can't help it. These words are coming out whether I want them to or not.

I grip the back of my neck and wince, my body resisting my stupid brain. "She's uh... She's kind of experienced when it comes to guys, right?"

"I don't really keep track, but yeah, I'm pretty sure

she's done it." Sammy's forehead is bunched tight when she glances up at me. "I didn't think that kind of thing would bother a stud muffin like you."

I hold my breath for a beat before spewing out my confession. "But I'm not."

Her eyes shoot up to meet mine. "What?"

"I'm not, Sam. I talk a big game, but I've never gone that far with a girl before."

Her eyes are so wide right now, I can clearly see faint green speckles in the royal blue of her irises. "You're a virgin?" she practically shouts.

I slap my hand over her mouth with a sharp scowl. "Could you say that any louder?"

"Sorry." Her words are muffled by my hand. "I'm just surprised."

Pulling my hand away with a heavy sigh, I cringe and look at the ground. "Why? We both know I'm an idiot."

Her long fingers brush my forearm. "You know I'm joking every time I say that, right?"

I gaze down at her hand, comforted by the soft touch.

"I've opened my big mouth too many times, trying to live up to my older brother and then the guys at school. Now if I ever try to get it on with a girl around here, she'll see right through me. My lies will be exposed and I don't know if I can face that." I glance up, my jaw working to the side. "I was just gonna wait until I moved away and went to college, but now I'm worried Roxy might expect a little more."

Sammy presses her lips together, her face wrinkling as she absorbs my confession. I don't even know why the hell I'm telling her. I obviously need to get it off my chest.

I hold my breath, nervously waiting her out, until she snorts and starts laughing. "I'm sorry. Oh, man. This must be killing you. The way you talk, I thought you were a total man-whore! But you're..." She tips her head and gives me an affectionate smile. "You know that's kinda cute, right?"

"Shut up, Sams." I push her shoulder and she falls back on her ass, still laughing.

Her long hair brushes the pavement as she leans on her elbow and shakes her head at me. "I can't believe it."

"Tell anyone and I will end you." I point at her.

Her laughter cuts off and she gives me an earnest look of promise. "You know I won't."

"Thank you," I whisper. I swear, if my cheeks get any hotter, I'm going to catch fire.

Slumping onto my butt, I rest my elbows on my knees

and look up at the cloudy sky. "What am I going to do?"

Sammy sits up too. Scratching the side of her nose, she clears her throat and looks me in the eye.

"I think you're right to wait. I mean, you want prom to be a night to remember...for all the *right* reasons. You shouldn't have to live up to my sister's expectations, which are always way too high, anyway. Just make sure you're hanging out with your crew the whole time. Don't put yourself in a position where expectations need to be met. If you want to leave Nelson with your rep intact then just keep playing those evasive maneuvers." Her lips purse to the side as she crosses her leg and starts splitting a piece of grass with her thumbnail. "You know, I think having sex for the first time is a really big deal. I don't want to experience that with someone I don't trust. That way, if it *is* totally embarrassing, which it probably will be, you can just laugh about it and keep practicing." She gives me a wicked grin and wiggles her eyebrows.

The look on her face kind of throws me for a second. I've never thought of Sammy as the kind of girl who would be into sex, but that smile, that hungry little glint in her eyes—there might be a little vixen in the skater girl after all.

The thought makes a broad smile pop onto my face and I can't help laughing. I like her take on it, the idea of figuring it out with someone you care about. Someone you can tell your darkest secrets to and they're not going to blab them to the school.

Kind of like the opposite of Roxy.

I glance at Sammy as she presses her cheek on the top of Axel's head and starts scratching his neck before wrapping her arms all the way around him. He leans into the embrace and I'm struck once again by how easy it is to be with her.

Kind of like the opposite of Roxy.

12

SNOOPING

SAMMY

TYLER'S A VIRGIN. Who knew such a small tidbit of information could make me feel so good. Or maybe it's the way he confessed it to me. I'm the only person on this planet who knows his truth, and it puts me in a very privileged position.

Thank God I didn't stonewall him when he showed up at the skate park with Axel. But I just couldn't resist that lovable dog… and Tyler's face. I had to reconnect with the guy. The only way I could think to do it was to hassle him about him sucking face with Roxy.

Can't believe it paid off.

Pushing open the front door, I carry my board up to my room and lean it against the wall. I can't stop shaking my head with relief. Tyler hasn't slept with my sister, and there's a strong chance he won't. Like he'd risk exposing himself to her gossipy little mouth. Man, I hope he stays strong. I'm not sure what she has in mind, but I wouldn't put it past her to try it just to annoy me.

Snatching my pillow off the floor, I throw it back onto my bed before pulling my crumpled duvet straight. What if she does take his first time?

Slumping onto the mattress, I nibble my thumbnail and force myself to imagine it. Not them actually doing it, but the repercussions of them doing it. Will it tear them apart because it was just way too awkward, or will my personal nightmare become a reality? Will sex with Roxy make Tyler fall in love with her?

After a few minutes of painful deliberation, I look down at my jagged nail edge and decide that no matter what, Roxy can't touch my friendship with Ty. And at the end of the day, that's more important to me than anything...and I'm not going to let whatever the hell they have going on, screw it up.

There's no point trying to compete for his affections. Having him sit there opening up to me made me realize this. I'd rather have Tyler as a buddy for life than a boyfriend for half a second. I just need to chill and stop worrying so much about the stupid prom. I wasn't even going to go anyway, so it's not like it affects me. Let

Tyler have his moment. As long as he's still around to skate with the next day, I'm cool with it.

I let out a breath and repeat my little mantra, "I'm cool with it. Totally cool with it." Standing up, I catch my reflection in the full-length mirror and flick my hands up. "I am!"

Turning away from what might be a lie, I step into the hallway and head for Roxy's room. Seeing Tyler reminded me that I need to borrow her camera and start snooping around the photography club. A little smile pushes at my lips.

Snooping. I love that word.

I knock and wait, leaning on the edge of my beat-up Vans while I listen for Roxy.

Nothing but crickets.

Leaning my ear against the wood, I hold the handle and do one more final check before easing her door open.

Yes. She's not home. Makes the whole camera-borrowing thing a million times easier.

Stepping into the pink tornado, I wrinkle my nose and head to her desk. I don't know where she keeps her camera, but her desk is as good a start as any. I begin with the top left drawer and work my way across, finally unearthing it in the bottom right corner.

Pulling it out, I brush the dust off and shake my head. Such a waste. Mom spent a fortune on this thing when Roxy was going through her photography phase and the stupid girl has hardly used it.

I unzip the padded case and pull out the camera. Turning it on, I take off the lens cap and raise it to my eye. I do a quick sweep of the room, impressed by the clarity, then snap a shot of Roxy's ballet shoe poster on the wall.

I check the display to see how it came out, but the photo disappears before I get a chance.

"O-kay. Um…" I scan the buttons and go for the most obvious choice, smiling when my photo pops up on display. "Nice. Crystal clear."

Without thinking, I press the arrow key and start scrolling through the images Roxy has taken. What can I say, I'm a curious chick.

I'm really doing it to prove that Roxy never uses the awesome stuff Mom buys her. I'm expecting images of that Christmas day and nothing else.

But I get *else*.

I get a whole lot of *else*.

Once I pass the ten fake *happy family* shots from Christmas day, my face bunches with confusion as I gaze at the first image to take me off guard. It's a page of writing. I squint, trying to make out the text. It looks like a girl's handwriting. I can't really read it on the tiny display screen. I think I can make out the name Anna in a couple of places, and there's a bunch of HANSON followed by exclamation marks. I'm not really sure what that's about.

I can't figure out how to bring up the time stamp on the photos, so I just keep flicking, hoping to come across some image that will give away the season or something.

"Writing. Writing. Writing," I mutter as I speed through page after page of text. I don't know why Roxy felt the need to photograph someone's notebook, but whatever. "Probably not the types of photos Mom was hoping for, Rox." I sneer and then freeze.

"What?" I can barely breathe as I'm struck by a new image that's making my stomach curdle. It's of these two guys getting it on with a dark-haired chick. Her sexy red dress is pushed off her shoulder, and the guy licking her skin has this wicked gleam in his eye.

Why the hell does Roxy have that on her camera?

I don't know where it was taken. I'm assuming a party. But when?

Pressing the arrow, I move onto the next shot and the next. They only get worse, and then they get freaking horrifying.

"Oh, shit," I whisper. "Layla."

Those guys are Derek and Quaid! I pull the camera closer to my face and suddenly recognize them. With the dark lighting, it was kind of hard to tell at first, but...

Eww!

This particular shot only shows the side of Layla's face, but it's so obviously her. These must be the photos Tyler was talking about. My heart starts pounding as I go through the rest of them.

I can't believe I've actually found them.

Glancing over my shoulder, I check the door, hoping the shuffling in the hallway isn't Roxy. I better hurry; if I get busted in here with this, she'll end me.

I'm still trying to wrap my brain around what I'm seeing...and why the hell these shots are on her camera. Did she take them?

As much as I dislike my sister, I'm really hoping someone borrowed it that night and that she's blissfully unaware of what's on here.

Breaths are punching out of me now—fast and erratic. I push the arrow and go still. It's another shot of Layla and the guys, but this one is different. Scarily so.

"Yes, Mom, I heard you!"

Roxy voice makes me gasp. Switching off the camera, I scramble to shove it back in its bag and tuck it away in the drawer. My frenetic movements nearly make me drop the thing. It clunks into the drawer and I slide it shut before bouncing up and making a beeline for her door. She hates me coming into her room.

I press my ear to the wood and am relieved to hear the toilet flushing. I make a quick escape and am caught closing Roxy's door.

"What are you doing? Were you just in my room?" Her dark hair falls over her shoulders as she storms toward me.

"No," I snap, then sigh. "Okay, fine. I was *about* to go in there."

"Why?" Roxy's eyes narrow.

"I want to borrow your camera." I say it casually, my eyes scrutinizing her face as I desperately look for clues.

She gives me nothing that I wouldn't expect. Her eyebrow arches and she starts shaking her head. "You know the answer's no."

"Come on, Rox. I just want to take a couple of pictures at the skate park. The guys are working on a new trick and—"

"No." She cuts me off like usual.

"Why?" I whine.

"Because Mom bought me that camera, and it's really expensive. I don't trust you to look after my stuff."

I look to the ceiling and groan. "One time, Rox!"

"That iPod was brand new!" She points at me. "You had it for, what? A day?"

"I was eight! It fell out of my pocket. How many times do I have to apologize for that?"

"You don't!" She puts her hands on her hips. "But I'm not lending you any more of my stuff."

"Gimme a break. When was the last time you even used it?" I snap, hoping she can't spot the pulse pounding in my neck.

Roxy thinks for a second then shrugs. "I don't know. Christmas, probably."

And there's the lie. Although she doesn't look as though she's lying. Maybe her camera *was* stolen and returned without her knowledge. Or maybe my sister is the world's best con artist.

I push for a little more, trying to trip her up. "So it's been stuck in your drawer for over four months? I'm sure Mom would love to hear that."

Roxy sticks her manicured nail in my face. "Tell her and

I'll blab about the time you stole her car for a chocolate fix."

"I borrowed it!"

"You were twelve!"

I huff and look to the ceiling. "Are we really going to play this game right now?"

"Actually, we don't need to, because we all know Mom's going to believe me over you."

My glare is dark as I level my eyes at her and grit out, "Just let me use your frickin' camera."

"No." She shakes her head again…still giving me nothing. She's not edgy or tense; she's looking me right in the eye as if she has nothing to hide. "Sam, seriously, you're one of the most irresponsible people I know. You're not borrowing my stuff!"

"Girls." Mom starts climbing the stairs. "What's going on?"

"Nothing." I let out a disgusted huff and push past my sister. I know when I've lost an argument, and like hell am I getting Mom involved. I'm not ready to start accusing Roxy of anything until I absolutely know the truth.

My sister may be manipulative and bitchy, but surely she wouldn't stoop so low as to stab her best friend in the back. I don't want to dump her in it if she's innocent.

But on the flip side, if she's guilty, exposing her will rain down all kinds of hell on people I actually care about. Roxy will not fall without a fight and if she's cornered, the first thing she'll do is lash out. I close my eyes, picturing the Nelson High hallways lined with images of Layla, Quaid, and Derek.

Closing my bedroom door, I sink to the floor and rest my elbows on my knees.

Tyler said the party paparazzo was a guy. I kind of like the idea of following that train of thought for now. Let's assume some douche took Roxy's camera.

Lightly thumping my head against the wood, I look to the posters on my ceiling with a sad frown. So how did some douche get into Roxy's room to take the thing?

My eyes slide shut as I swallow down the bile in my throat. Denying the inevitable is going to be damn hard. The only people who are ever allowed in Roxy's room are Layla and... Michelle.

We all know Layla didn't do it, so that leaves the cheer-leading bimbo.

Maybe she's not as clueless as we all assume.

13

KICKFLIP MISHAP

TYLER

I BALANCE my skateboard on the edge of the ramp and wait for Sammy to finish her trick before dipping into the descent. I love that initial fall and the way your body feels as you swing back up the other side. Going back and forth a few times, I build up speed before grinding the bar and then dropping down again. I kind of want to copy what Sammy did a minute ago with the under-coping invert, where she placed her hand on the ramp and grabbed her board before sliding back into the fall. It was way cool, but I don't want to make a total ass of myself.

I stick with a simple stall, then drop back in for my last run. Sammy's standing on the top, watching me with a glazed expression. Something's up with her today.

When I texted her to come meet me she seemed normal, but as soon as she arrived I knew something was off. After our deep and meaningful convo yesterday, I'm not overly keen on diving into another. I couldn't stop thinking about her last night, and it weirded me out big time.

But I don't like the idea that something's eating her up. She seems tense and unhappy.

And I need to figure out why.

As soon as I finish my run Sammy kicks off on hers, denying me the chance to chat. She's doing simple moves, so I figure she can probably concentrate and talk at the same time. It might actually be easier to get whatever out of her if she's focusing on her board and not me. It's less intimate that way.

"So, how was your night?"

"You know." She shrugs, her eyes on the ramp as she comes up to meet me and then drops back down. Her hair flies behind her as she picks up speed. It's getting kind of long now. I wonder if she ever brushes it. It's so fine and silky she probably doesn't even need to.

I frown.

Why the hell am I thinking about Sammy's hair?

Shaking my head, I focus back on my friend. "You okay, man? You seem kind of quiet."

She glances up and we make swift eye contact as she crests the ramp, then flicks the board beneath her and drops back down. "I know we had deep chats yesterday, dude, but I'm not after a repeat. Now shut up and let me concentrate."

"That's cool." I raise my hand, smelling her lie and wondering how far to push her. Maybe talking about something else will make something slip.

I let a few minutes pass, focusing on the rhythmic slide and click of Sammy's board before blurting, "So, any luck with the photography club thing?"

Sammy's hitting the top of the ramp when I ask, attempting a kickflip rock-n-roll. It's a tough trick, but she's been doing it for a few months now. I expect her to spin the board and land with ease, but it doesn't quite work out that way.

"Ahhh!" she cries as the board flies out from under her and she hits the ramp with a smack. She slides down to the middle and rolls away from me.

I wince and hiss, ready to give her some sympathy... expecting her to stand and mutter a few curses before trying again.

But she doesn't come up.

My stomach catapults into my throat.

"Sammy?"

Jumping down the ramp, I hit the smooth surface and slide on my knees until I'm right behind her.

"You okay?"

She's cradling her arm against her chest, the fingers of her left hand locked around her right wrist. Her teeth are clamped together and her face is scrunched tight in pain.

"Sammy," I whisper, leaping over her so I can roll her onto her back.

She whimpers and squeezes her eyes shut.

"Is it your wrist?"

Her shoulders hitch with a shrug then she starts nodding. "It frickin' hurts, man."

The words sound broken and wispy, and it makes something in my chest pull tight. I rest my hand on her neck and run my thumb along the edge of her jaw.

"It's gonna be okay." Wrenching the phone from my back pocket, I quickly find Mack's number. He lives closest to the park...and he's got the fastest car.

He makes me wait four rings, which feels like a freaking eternity.

"Hey, man. Can I call you ba—"?

"No, I need you now. Sam's hurt. I've got to get her to the hospital."

There's a micro-pause before he answers, "I'll be there in two minutes."

Shoving my phone away, I lean over Sam and study her face, trying to read how much pain she's in. I'm not used to seeing her like this. She's a tough nugget. The best skater I know. I've seen her fall before, but she always gets up.

She squirms on the ramp, hissing as she tries to sit. I glide my arm around her shoulders for support, coaxing her into leaning against me. She resists me at first, then kind of relaxes against my chest.

I don't know what to say to make it feel better. Asking her if it still hurts is stupid. I can see how much it's hurting. So I just sit there while we wait, gently holding her and experiencing this protective kind of instinct I'm not used to.

I guess I kind of felt it when Braxton first moved in. He was a fragile kid, and we were all overprotective of the little guy.

But I've never felt this way about, well, Sammy before.

I kind of don't know what to do with it.

The roar of Mack's engine reaches us before we see

him. As soon as I hear the rumble, I jump to my feet and bend down to scoop Sammy up.

"What are you doing?" she snaps, pushing me away with her good arm. "Don't be a dick, man. I can walk to the car."

Stepping back with a dry sigh, I gently pull her left arm until she's standing beside me.

"Can you grab my board?"

I kind of want to hover beside her as she shuffles to Mack's Camaro, but after her little shove away, I hardly think she's looking for some kind of knight. Securing her board will mean a hell of a lot more to her than guiding her to the car.

I run back and snatch up both boards, then race over the grass. Mack's already standing by the passenger door, flipping the front seat forward so I can jump into the back. I nestle the boards at my feet while Sammy eases into the front.

I reach around her for the seatbelt, ignoring her huff as I click it in for her. I usually love her fierce independence. Today, it's a pain in the ass. She needs to let me help her. *I* need to help her.

Perching my butt on the edge of the seat, I stretch forward and rest my hand on her shoulder. Why I feel the overwhelming need to stay connected, I'm not sure.

"What happened?" Mack checks the street and pulls onto the quiet road.

"Screwed up a kickflip on the ramp," Sammy grumbles, then thumps her head back against the headrest. "Dammit. Mom's gonna be so pissed."

"How's the pain now?" I ask.

"Still there." Her voice is unusually quiet, her strong face looking pale and slightly fragile.

I rub her shoulder and will Mack to move a little faster.

He catches my eye in the rearview mirror. I don't know what he's thinking, but there's a little glint in them that I can't be bothered deciphering.

Just get us to the damn hospital, man!

I clench my jaw and mutter under my breath as we get to an intersection and slow for the yellow light.

"Seriously?" I smack his shoulder. "She's in pain here."

He swivels to look into the back. "Exactly. You want her having another accident on the way to the hospital?"

I huff and look up at the lights, silently begging them to turn green. As soon as it changes, I yell at Mack, "Go, go, go!"

He eases through the intersection and continues to

drive like a grandma to the hospital, taking extra care at each stop sign and four-way crossing.

"You're frickin' killing me," I mumble.

I'm not sure if he hears me or not. If he does, he doesn't respond. Pulling into the hospital, he accelerates to the emergency room and jumps out of the car, running around to open Sammy's door.

Placing his hand under her elbow, he steadies her while I scramble out of the car.

"I'll meet you in there," he calls over his shoulder

I usher Sammy into the ER. She's still being really quiet, which tells me how bad she must be feeling. I snatch a glimpse of her pale complexion and my insides fold.

Always so brave and tough.

She never gives the world anything, but I can see that pain in her blue eyes and it makes me start calling for a doctor the second we make it through those sliding glass doors.

14

THE RANT CUTOFF

SAMMY

TYLER'S FUSSING. It's so unlike him I don't even know what to do with it.

"She needs to see a doctor right now. She's in pain." His strong finger jabs the glossy countertop while an unimpressed receptionist looks him over.

"Fill this out and we'll see her as soon as we can."

"That's not good enough," he barks.

"It's fine." Forcing a smile, I take the clipboard and walk to a nearby chair. My arm is freaking killing me, but I put on a brave face and start trying to fill out the form with my left hand.

It only takes thirty seconds for Tyler to snatch it out of

my grasp and start filling in the details. It's kind of cool that he knows them all without me having to tell him. He even remembers my birthday.

I watch over his shoulder, resisting the urge to lean my head against him. It was actually kind of nice having him hold me steady while I sat on the skate ramp, my mind trying to counter the pain traveling up my arm.

I'm guessing I've broken something, which totally sucks because Mom already hates me skating as it is. Thank God Dad's in Denver this week. I don't want to think about what kind of argument my accident will cause.

"You gotta sign it," Tyler mumbles, holding the board for me while I scribble this pathetic-looking signature.

Mack appears just as Tyler's rising from his chair. "Here, I'll take it."

He walks it up to the counter while Tyler turns to face me. "You doing okay?"

"Yeah, it's probably just a break. No big deal."

His expression warns me it's a huge deal.

I turn away from him and look across the sea of plastic chairs. They're all fused together and lined up in rows, filled with everything from sniveling kids to an old guy who's fallen asleep. A baby cry comes from the back corner, this pitiful little wail that's kind of grating.

My arm now has a pulse. It's thumping with this angry vibe that's telling me off for not concentrating through the trick. Tyler's question threw me. It shouldn't have, but it did, because I have a little truth nugget that I'm not ready to share with him and it's eating me alive.

Mack takes a seat on the other side of me. "Do you want me to call your mom?"

"No." I shake my head. "She'll just come down here and start fussing." I throw a glance at Tyler before turning to Mack and whispering, "And we've kind of got enough of that right now."

Mack snickers and whispers back, "It's only cause he cares about you."

The sentiment stumps me and I have to snigger, "Whatever."

I look away from Mack before he can see how warm those words make me. Turning back to Ty, I give him this sad kind of smile, which he mirrors. "Don't worry, Skater Girl. You'll be back on your board in no time."

I grin at his effort. "Thanks, man."

I have to admit, I kind of love that he's here, although he'd no doubt rather be hanging out with my sister than spending time in a noisy emergency room.

Ignoring the sting of that thought, I lean my head back

against the wall and try to focus on anything other than the angry pulse in my arm.

———

"The doctor will be with you in just a few minutes." The nurse smiles at me before padding out of the room.

We had to wait nearly an hour. One of the nurses came over to give me some Tylenol while I waited...only after Tyler got kind of pissy with her. He must have walked back and forth to that counter about ten times while we waited for my turn.

I've never seen him like this before. He's even followed me into the exam room.

"You don't have to stay."

He stops pacing and smiles at me. "No, I want to."

"Yeah, right. Seriously, dude, just go. I'm fine."

"You're not fine, Sammy. You're hurt!" He points at my arm, which I haven't stopped cradling since I hit that ramp.

"Yeah, but it's most likely just a break. Sure, it hurts, but it's not like I'm dying. Wouldn't you rather be out...picking flowers for my sister or something?"

Even saying that makes my throat burn.

Does Roxy deserve flowers?

Man, I wish I knew.

I look away from Tyler's incredulous expression. "I'm not exactly the flower-picking kind, Sam."

"Yeah, well, maybe you should start. Chicks love that kind of thing." I kick my legs, watching them swing as I wait for the slow-ass doctor to get here.

I can't imagine a guy ever picking me flowers, let alone buying them. The thought kind of stings. I don't want to be one of those girls like Roxy, but that doesn't mean I want to turn into some lonely cat lady, either.

Squeezing my eyes shut, I try to ward off these sudden feelings. I hate how vulnerable being hurt makes me feel. I don't want to be girly about it. And I sure as hell don't want to start crying, but my eyes are doing that burning thing again.

"Seriously, Ty. Just go."

"I'm not leaving." His voice, although quiet, is really firm, and it riles me.

"It's a Sunday. The sun is shining, the sky is blue. Go enjoy it. Spend time with your awesome family. Do something! It's better than pacing around this sterile room with some invalid."

With a sharp huff, Tyler storms towards me and stops

against the bed. "Sammy, get this through your head. There's nowhere else I want to be right now. If I wasn't here, and I found out what had happened to you, I would leave wherever I was to come make sure you were okay. Don't you get that?"

"No! I don't get that!" I thunder as something inside of me breaks open, unleashing a mouthful of drivel. "People don't drop what they're doing for me. Why the hell do you think I have to be so independent all the time? I can't afford to rely on anyone. Dad is always away. Mom is always busy with some charity or Roxy event. My sister doesn't give a shit about me. I am *used* to looking after myself, and I don't want to have to rely on you!" I huff. "So just go!" I point to the door.

He doesn't move. Instead, he tortures me by studying my face with those gorgeous eyes of his. His eyebrows bunch for a second before he softly murmurs, "It doesn't have to be like that, Sam."

"It *does* have to be like that." I close my eyes and shake my head. "What happens when you fall in love, huh? You're not going to be interested in skating with me anymore. And your girlfriend is not going to want you standing in an examination room with me. What do you think Roxy's going to say when she knows you spent all day with me instead of taking her out?"

"She won't—"

"And it's not like *I'm* ever going to get a boyfriend." I keep ranting, ignoring the warning bells in my head. The stupid injury is turning my brain to a lump of incompetent mush. "I'm a tomboy who can hit harder than most of the guys at our school. No one wants to date that. I don't even know how to wear makeup. I barely brush my hair. The last time I wore a dress, I was five years old. I'm barely a girl. Who's going to want to kiss me, huh? The only time these lips have touched flesh is when I was dared to kiss a stranger my freshman year! Twenty seconds of awkward lip-locking is hardly something to shout about." I let out a disgusted huff. "I'm nothing, man, and no one's ever going to look at me like I'm pretty or treat me like I'm special. No guy's ever gonna gaze into my eyes then press his mouth against—"

Tyler grabs my face. Brushing his thumbs over my cheekbones, he stares down at me before shutting me up with a firm kiss. My eyes bulge the second our lips connect, my body going stiff with shock.

What the hell is he doing?

… I really like it.

That thought seems to float through me, gliding into my bloodstream until I relax into the kiss. He's going to pull away any second now, so I need to savor this.

Kissing's always intrigued me, my twenty-second dare

not quite enough to satisfy my curiosity. I've watched couples lost in the moment, their mouths and breaths mingling as they get all tongue-tied. I always thought it looked kind of sloppy. But this... I've never felt a sensation like it before. It's soft and smooth, firm yet also kind of pliant. Tyler's fingers curl into my hair, sending spikes of pleasure running down my neck. Tipping my head to the side, I press back, then suck his bottom lip into my mouth. I don't even know what possesses me to do it. It just seems like the natural play.

Tyler's fingers tighten against my neck and all of a sudden his tongue sweeps inside my mouth, convincing me that this whole kissing thing might be something I need to investigate further, because holy shit... It feels freaking amazing!

15

PRINCESS SAMMY

TYLER

I SHOULD BE PULLING AWAY RIGHT NOW. I don't even know why I'm kissing Sammy in the first place. I just couldn't stand that rant anymore. I had to lay one on her. To convince her that she wasn't all boy.

And now I don't want to stop.

She feels good. Her tongue is like... Oh, man.

And her lips are just...

And then she sucked my lip into her mouth and I was like...

My brain isn't working right. I can't think past the feel of Sam's tongue in my mouth. The sweet sensation of her luscious lips working with mine to create some kind of awesome magic.

I've kissed plenty of girls before.

But this is something else.

It's not hungry or anxious, lusty or sweet... It's just this natural awesomeness that I can't stop tasting.

"Miss Carmichael?" The doctor's voice tears us apart. I leap away from Skater Girl, nearly falling into the chair next to the bed. I right myself and give the doctor a sheepish grin.

He smirks at me. "I'm sorry, am I interrupting something?"

"No." I clear my throat and point at my friend. "Please."

He smiles and stands in front of Sammy. "I'm Dr. Thompson. Let me have a look at that arm of yours."

Sammy doesn't say much during the examination...and she won't look at me, either. She just answers each question in monotone and is then taken away for X-rays. I try to follow her, but the doc tells me to wait.

So I start pacing. I walk from one side of the small cubicle to the other, rubbing my finger over my bottom lip and reliving every sensation of that kiss. Gripping the back of my neck, I stare at the floor and try to figure out what I'm supposed to do with it.

It was a total act of impulse. I assumed it would just be a little peck, but her lips were so pliable. They tasted so sweet. I had to have more.

I'm kind of bummed out that Sammy wouldn't look at me after. I mean, I get it. We're friends, skating buddies, pals since we were seven. It's way awkward to go kissing her.

Brushing my thumb over my lip, I try to convince myself that I shouldn't want to do it again. I'm kind of with Roxy. I can't go messing around with Sam, and there's no way I'm breaking my date to prom.

One, it'll make me look like a total loser and two, everyone with any kind of brain knows you don't piss off Roxanne Carmichael. If I'm trying to make a better name for myself, I need to hold off until after prom.

That'll give me time to decide how I really feel.

Maybe this was just a spur-of-the-moment thing. Maybe when I wake up tomorrow, I won't feel like a repeat.

Scratching the back of my head, I walk back out to the waiting room to check in with Mack. His ankle is perched on his knee while he flips through a magazine.

I lightly kick his foot and plop into the chair beside him.

"All good?" He slaps the magazine shut and drops it back on top of the pile stacked on the table next to him.

"Yeah, she's gone for X-rays and then they'll set it in plaster."

"We should probably be calling her parents."

"Yeah, I know." I sigh. "But she didn't want me to."

"Fine, but who's going to pay the bill when we leave?"

I groan and pull out my phone, finding Sammy's home number. I'm expecting Mrs. Carmichael to answer, so I'm a little stumped when Roxy's voice comes down the line. Since when does she answer her home phone?

"Hello?" Her voice is short and clipped.

"Oh, uh, hey, Rox." I smile, but it feels tight and forced.

Mack's eyes are on me, so I swivel away. He's been pretty impartial about me taking Roxy to prom. We haven't really talked about it; the guy's kind of obsessed with New Zealand right now, and there's not much room for other conversation. Just quietly, it's getting old real fast.

"Hey, Tyler." She sounds kind of bored but then perks up. "So, what are you doing? Please tell me you're not skating at the park with Sammy. Why don't you come hang out with me instead?"

"I'm at the hospital with Sammy. They think she's broken her arm."

"Really?" Roxy's voice pitches. "Is she okay?"

"Yeah, she's gonna be fine, but I thought I better let your parents know."

"Dad's out of town. I'll give Mom a call." She hangs up without saying goodbye and I'm back to playing the waiting game.

Sliding the phone away, I look at Mack, hoping he can't figure out what Sammy and I got up to in the examination room.

"She coming?"

"It was Rox. She's going to call her mom."

He nods. "Sammy'll be pissed, but it's the right move."

"You can go if you want, man. I can call my dad to come get me."

"Nah, that's cool." Mack lightly smacks my shoulder with the back of his hand. "I don't mind kicking around with you. I want to make sure Sammy's good before leaving." He shuffles in his seat. "Although, she's gonna be fine. That girl is one tough chick. Can't imagine anything ever beating her."

I snicker and scratch my eyebrow. I used to think that was true. But the look in her eyes when she started ranting makes me wonder. The way she let me kiss her... I have to consider the fact that for all Sammy's hard-ass coating, maybe there's a girl under there who just wants someone to make her his number one priority. Maybe she does want that knight to ride into the sunset with. I grin. He may not be allowed to carry her to his horse, but maybe there *is* a little princess in Sammy after all.

And I seriously don't know what to do with that.

16

THE JUDGMENT ZONE

SAMMY

SO IT'S safe to say things have been weird since the whole hospital-kissing thing. I kind of don't know what to do with it.

Tyler stuck around at the hospital while I got my arm plastered. It's now in a sling—painful and annoying. I can't skate. I can't bike. And Mom's pretty much read me the riot act every day this week. I'm not sure how much more I can take.

The thing that's driving me the most nuts though is my obsession with Tyler's kiss. I can't stop thinking about it, and I really should because the only reason he did it was to make me feel better. That's the kind of guy he is. He hates emotional angst and he'll do anything to put a quick stop to it. Usually, he'd feed me some one-liner or make me crack up laughing with a stupid facial expression or joke, but no, he decided to play the kiss move and it was totally unfair.

Part of me wants to tell him how I feel about him. That way he'll know not to go messing with me again. But if I do that, things will get awkward between us, and they're already bad enough. We've barely looked at each other since we lip-locked. We still chat, raise our chins in greeting as we pass in the hallway, but it's obvious we're both avoiding each other.

All I can hope for is that within a few days everything will settle down. Prom's this weekend. Roxy can distract him with her infuriating charm and then Tyler and I can go back to being what we were: buddies who like to hang out. That easy, no-fuss friendship that I treasure so much. We can pretend the kiss never happened, and the only trouble I'll be left with is the whole *what the hell were those pictures doing on Roxy's camera* thing.

I haven't made it back into her room to get those photos yet. With my arm in a cast, Mom's been acting like the nurse from hell, treating me like I can't do a damn thing without her. Trying to time it so I'm actually alone in the house has been impossible.

I'm still not even sure if I should get them. I mean, I should. They're evidence, right? But evidence against who?

A snapshot of Layla's face flashes through my mind.

My forehead wrinkles with unease.

I've been keeping a close eye on Michelle this week. She's acting just like Rox—irritatingly innocent. She doesn't usually spare much time for me, so rolling on up and starting a conversation is going to look way suspicious. Instead, I've just been doing the stalker thing and kind of following her around the school.

Right now, she's strutting down the hallway. Her blonde curls have been French braided around the bottom of her head and then left to roam free over her shoulder. I look down as she passes me, feeling like Diana Rowden. She's the female spy I'm researching for my world history assignment. Yes, thanks to Tori's nagging, I finally picked a topic. It's actually really interesting. Those female spies were freaking kick-ass.

Michelle's hips swivel as she rounds the corner and prances toward the cafeteria, where she'll take her perch next to Roxy and all I'll be able to do is watch them from afar. What I really want is to spot Michelle with a camera in her hands, or overhear her say something completely suspicious so I can jump on it. But she's not playing fair.

Adjusting my sling, I turn away and head for the front entrance. I'm not really in the mood to endure lunch in that noisy cafeteria. Plus, I don't want to watch my sister flirt with Tyler. With prom only a few days away, she's really turned up the heat. He seems to be going with it, which hurts like a hot poker in the eye, but it's what he wants. I'm the one he kisses to shut up, and Roxy's the one he kisses to make himself feel good. I just have to accept it and move on.

The sun is shining outside. It's a good day to sit in the grass...or run home and get those photos.

I'm trying to calculate how long it will take me to get there, sneak into Roxy's room, and run back to school. I also need to consider the fact that Mom might walk in the door while I'm doing it.

Did she say she was out this morning or this afternoon?

How fast will I have to run to make it there and back again? Is it worth the risk?

Yes.

Flicking my hair over my shoulder, I pick up my pace but am stopped short by the last person I'm expecting to see.

"Kiwi Girl?"

She's currently flanked by Finn and Layla, and she's looking both excited and petrified. Her long hair is tied back in a messy bun and she looks like she hasn't slept in a couple of days. Long-haul flying really sucks it out of you, I guess. In spite of her pale, tired complexion, she's still stunning.

It's not fair, but at least she's nice.

"Hey, Sam." Her smile is tired but still beautiful.

I saunter over to her, a smirk forming on my lips. "What are you doing here?"

"Surprising Mack. Can't have the guy missing his last prom because he doesn't have a date." She flicks a curl off her cheek and pulls in a breath. She looks like she's prepping for battle. But there's also a glint of excitement running through her green eyes.

Seriously, her insides must be a mess of knots right now. The cloud she left under was black and overflowing with scandal. Yeah, Mack flew to New Zealand and made it all right again, but none of the other students at Nelson High went with him. This will be their first sight of her again since reading that ugly cartoon.

Murdering little slut.

That's what the person who outed Kaija had called her, and by the nervous look on Layla's face and the shadow of fear crossing Kaija's expression, they're both still worried it's gonna stick.

"Love makes people do crazy shit," I mutter.

My comment makes Finn laugh, the deep, rich sound shattering the thick tension around us. Layla looks at him, letting out a nervous giggle, which Kaija picks up on too. It's that crazy kind of laughter, borderline psych-ward, but it's pretty damn funny.

I grin as I watch them trying to battle their nerves, and I totally change my mind about the whole avoiding the cafeteria thing. The photos will have to wait. I cannot miss this.

"You're one brave chick, Kaija. I'm digging it."

Kaija tips her head toward Layla. "It was her idea."

It's impossible to mask my surprise. I thought Layla hated the kiwi invasion. I look from her to Kaija, then up to Finn. He just nods and gives me this secretive kind of grin. Okay, more backstory I don't understand. Whatever.

"What happened to your arm?" Kaija points to the black sling that's digging into the side of my neck. I seriously hate this thing.

I make a face. "Came off my board. Fractured one of my wrist bones. It's not too bad. Should be out of this thing before summer break."

"Still a total drag though, right?"

"You know it."

Kaija's eyes sparkle as she gives me a friendly smile. "Bet it won't stop you skating."

All I can do is smirk.

She laughs at me, then looks at Layla. "Okay, let's do this."

"Just focus on the fact that you'll be surprising your boyfriend." She holds up a square box that looks suspiciously like bakery food. "Keep your eyes on him and everything else can just disappear." Layla nudges Kaija's arm and gives her a kind smile. I've been seeing a lot more of those on her lately and they're really pretty. Finn's brought out the beautiful in that girl.

I glance at him while he stares down at Layla. She doesn't know it because she's too busy giving Kaija a little pep talk, but Finn is totally loving on his girl right now. It's almost barf-worthy, but because I like the guy so much I'm going to let him get away with it.

Spinning on my heel, I step in time with the trio, unable to fight my smile as I picture Mack's face when he sees Kaija walk in. I'm stoked I'm not missing this.

Things go quiet when we make the final turn towards the cafeteria. It's easy enough to walk through empty hallways, I guess, but to enter the judgment zone is kind of terrifying. I glance at Kaija's face, noting the set of her jaw and the way her nose is twitching. She's having an internal freak-out. And she's kind of justified. Last time she walked these halls they were plastered with incriminating cartoons of what she'd done to her friend back in New Zealand.

Not an easy thing to live down.

The fact she's even willing to return shows how much guts she has.

She slows to a stop outside the double doors. If I squint, I'm pretty sure I can see the vein in her neck pulsing. "You know, maybe I should just wait for him at home."

I reach in front of Finn and lightly tap her arm. "No way! Don't freak out. It's gonna be cool."

Her head bobs erratically.

"Trust me, you want to get the gasping out of the way *before* prom."

She turns to me, her eyes narrowing at the corners. "You just want to see Mack's face when I walk in."

"Yeah, pretty much." I arch my eyebrow and give her a mischievous smile. "Don't suppose you brought any cupcakes with you."

She laughs. "Actually, I did."

"No way!" My eyes bulge.

Layla gently wiggles the box and sings, "Promposal time."

Ugh. Those things are always so cheesy.

But Layla looks too pumped and Kaija's blushing too red for me to say anything other than, "Good luck. You can do it."

Kaija sucks in the breath and holds it.

"Hey." I nudge her arm until she's looking at me again. "Hold your head high. All the important people in that room know the real truth, and we all think you're cool. Screw the rest of them—they can think whatever the hell they like. It won't change the fact you get to play tongue twister with Mack Mahoney after school today."

Kaija's head droops forward and her shoulders start shaking. I give her a quizzical frown until her head pops up and she lets her laughter loose again. "Thanks, Sammy. That's just what I needed to hear."

"Good." I step back, then tip my head toward the door. "Now, go shock the hell out of your boyfriend."

"With pleasure," she whispers before giving me one last nervous smile and following Layla and Finn into the cafeteria.

17

THE RETURN OF THE CUPCAKES

TYLER

ROXY'S HAND is on my shoulder, her painted nails digging into my shirt as she laughs at something Michelle said. I don't know what it was. I switched off as soon as I heard the words *designer* and *ode gucci*.

She's been hanging out with me a lot this week.

It's not so bad. She's hot. Her kisses are like fire, and I kind of like that.

I'd probably like it even more if thoughts of Sammy didn't try to invade my mind every time Roxy's lips touch mine.

I can't help thinking how different my lunch would be if I were kicking it with Sammy right now. We'd be talking about boarding or gaming...or something interesting. Shit, I'd even take a World War II convo over fashion speak.

Glancing sideways, I spot Layla approaching the table. Finn's behind her and I think there's someone behind him, but I don't lean over to see because I'm too busy glaring at the box in Layla's hands.

She places it on the table in front of Mack.

"Cupid's Bakery?" I read the label, still remembering the horror of biting into the world's foulest cupcake.

Kaija and Sammy pranked the whole team with those things. They were spicy devil cakes that nearly made half the team throw up.

"Are you shitting me right now, Lay-Lay?" Mack snickers. "What the hell is this?"

She gives him a cute little smirk, resting her hip against the table and looking kind of triumphant.

His expression is skeptical as he looks over his sister's shoulder to check with Finn.

"It's cool, man." Finn nods, his deep voice shaking just a little.

What is with his smile?

I frown and glance over my shoulder. Sammy's hovering near the door, her gaze on Mack. There's a sparkle in her eye, and I nearly reach across the table and slam my hand on the box.

I'm not letting Mack get burned again.

But I'm too late.

He's already looking inside, his forehead wrinkled.

"What is it?" I spin the box without asking permission and look at the neat rows of orange and blue cupcakes, each with an icing letter.

W—A—N—T

2—G—O—2

P—R—O—M?

I snicker and push the box back. "Has word not spread? Who's dumb enough to ask you to prom?"

"I am."

The female voice hits everyone before she steps around Finn and smiles down at Mack.

Roxy's fingers dig into my shoulder as I glance up at Kiwi Girl.

No freaking way.

Layla giggles as she stares at Mack's face.

He hasn't said anything yet. He's too busy gaping at his girlfriend like he can't quite believe she's here. But then he busts out in the biggest smile I've ever seen. It takes over his entire face. Rising from his seat, he walks around to her with this dopey grin and rests his hand on the side of her face before planting his lips on her smile.

I can't help a soft snicker. If this were a movie, people would be cheering right now. But it's not. It's high school, and the only sound to back up the loved-up couple is a torrent of whispers that rips through the cafeteria like a forest fire.

Mack and Kaija are oblivious to it.

Kiwi Girl's hands glide around Mack's waist and up his back while he holds her face and kisses the breath out of her. It makes me think of kissing Sammy.

I look away and spot Colt. He's looking over his shoulder, grinning at Tori, who's sitting with her best friend Amy and a pale-looking Anderson Foster. His lips have dropped into an over-sized O-shape and he's blinking like he can't quite compute what's going down. Tori is grinning and clapping her hands in this fast, frenetic way. "Yay," she mouths to her boyfriend, whose smile only increases the longer he stares at her.

I steal a glance at Sammy. I don't know why. I guess I'm just compelled to look at her for some reason. The second our eyes brush we both snap our heads away. Is she thinking about our kiss too?

Scratching the back of my neck, I pick up my fork and lightly tap it against the edge of my plate. My jaw works to the side as I try to ignore how awkward things are between us right now.

It's only then I become aware of how tight Roxy's grip is getting. Her breathing is kind of loud in my ear too. Subtly turning my head, I spy her out of the corner of my eye. Flaring nostrils, tight jaw.

What the hell's her problem?

So Kaija showed up for prom. Now Mack can come with us. I thought that'd be a good thing.

Gliding my arm around her waist, I give her a little squeeze and kiss the side of her face. Her response is a reluctant smile until she spots something over my shoulder. I'm about to turn to see what she's looking at, but she stops me with a hand on my cheek and starts making out with me right at the table.

I guess Mack's not the only one who can score some candy at the lunch table.

I go with it.

Why not, right?

It's not like I can get up from the table, march over to

Sammy and start kissing her like I did at the hospital. If things were awkward now, how much worse would they be if I tried to make a play for her?

I kissed her that day to try and wipe that look out of her eyes.

I didn't expect to like it so much.

All I can do now is make the most of what I have. I wanted Roxy Carmichael as my date to the prom, and I got her. This Saturday is going to be the best night of my life.

18

THE ROXY ROOM INVASION

SAMMY

ROXY LEFT straight from school to do more prom prep. Seriously, if the girl put as much time into her schoolwork as she did into organizing her precious prom outfit, she would have gotten into the New York Design School she wanted. Instead, she was moving up to Portland to hang out with Mom's sister for a year and help out at her boutique fashion shop.

As much as I can't wait to see Roxy go, I also am not looking forward to all of Mom's attention focused on me. Senior year has the potential to suck.

But I can't think about that now.

The house is empty, and now is my chance to sneak into Roxy's room and grab those photos. I put music on in my room, blasting it so that if Mom comes back early, she'll think I'm in my room.

Pink's voice floods the upstairs while I race into my sister's room. Running to her desk, I pull out the bottom drawer and reach in for the camera.

That's when the music clicks off.

"Samantha?" Mom calls.

"Shit," I mutter, quickly slamming the drawer shut again.

I have time to stand up and spin around, casually leaning against Roxy's desk as Mom walks in.

"Okay, one, your music was loud enough to wake the state of Idaho and two, what are you doing in Roxanne's bedroom?"

"Um..." I lick my lips, wanting to ask her why she's home and how the hell she snuck in so quietly. "I thought you were out."

"I just walked in."

"Oh." I nod. Dammit! "I didn't hear you."

"Yes, well, how could you?"

I scratch my eyebrow, looking at the floor to avoid her pointed glare. "Sorry about that." Hopefully, my apology is enough to let her drop the Roxy room invasion...but it's not.

"Now, what are you doing in here?"

"I just..." I shrug, pushing off Roxy's desk and heading for the door. Mom should step aside as I approach. "I was, um, looking for...some study notes."

"Study notes?" Mom's plucked eyebrows pucker.

"Yeah, I'm working on that history assignment and I can't remember how to do a proper...you know... What are they called? The thing at the back where you list the websites and books and stuff."

"A reference."

I snap my fingers and point at Mom with an innocent smile. It's probably more relieved than innocent, actually. I'm just glad I've come up with a plausible excuse. "That's the one. Anyway, I figured Roxy might have an assignment I could borrow and copy the formatting and stuff."

"She probably does, but you know how she is about her privacy. So you're going to have to wait until she gets home and ask her then."

I nod and finish my approach. Mom still hasn't moved. "Or you could just Google it."

"Good idea." My voice pitches. "That's brilliant. I don't know why I didn't think of that."

"Maybe it's because you're lying." She crosses her arms, her eyebrow peaking just the way Roxy's does.

My shoulders slump with a groan. "Okay, fine…"

Think, Sammy. Think!

"I was looking for something to wear."

What are you doing? You idiot!

I ignore myself and plow ahead when I see Mom's lips rise into a hopeful smile.

"I didn't want to admit it to you because I'm embarrassed, but there's this guy at school I kind of like, and I thought Roxy might have a nice top or something I could borrow. I don't know, it's dumb. I probably couldn't catch his eye if I tried. I just…"

"Oh, yes, you can! Sweetheart!" Mom rubs my arms excitedly, bustling into the room and going to Roxy's dresser drawers. "I'm sure there's something in here Roxy wouldn't mind you using. It's all for a good cause, right?" Mom winks and giggles.

Obviously Roxy's privacy is worthless when it comes to a fashion emergency.

I have to get out of this. I can*not* spend my afternoon stuck in my sister's pink nightmare, trying on clothes I hate while my mother fusses. She's already muttering to herself.

"No, wrong coloring for your skin tone." She pauses, eyes me up and down and then starts rummaging again. "Maybe a nice purple…but with the cast." She tsks. "We could easily cover that up, though."

As soon as she says the word makeup, I back into the doorframe. "Shoot, is that the time?" I glance at the watch I'm not wearing. "I thought it was earlier. I gotta go."

"Where?"

"To catch up with some friends."

"Is he going to be there?" Mom's face is so bright and expectant. Why can't she look at me this way when I'm just being myself?

I shake the thought off and force a smile. "Quite possibly."

"Well, don't you want to get changed first?"

"No, I'll save it for next time. I don't want to be late." I make a beeline for the stairs.

"Okay, sweetheart, I'll pick you out something pretty. You're going to knock this guy off his feet." I'm at the bottom of the stairs when she calls out again. "No bike or board! Do you want me to drive you?"

"No!" I practically shout. "It's not far, I'll just walk."

"Okay, I'll see you later."

I close the door on her next statement. If she really wants me to know it, she'll text. Sneaking around to the side of the house, I grab the spare board I keep hidden behind the shed and make sure I'm well clear of the Foster's place before placing it on the sidewalk and skating away.

I'm pretty sure I heard Tori mention something about a friendly football game after school at Connor's Park. She invited me, but I declined because of my photo mission. Well, that was a bust, so I may as well go hang out with my friends. I wonder if Tyler's there and I can't decide if I want him to be or not.

Watching him make out with Roxy in the cafeteria yesterday totally sucked. She's on him like a rash whenever I see them together. I'm beginning to think more and more that she's doing it to rile me, but if I'm stupid enough to watch them going mouth-to-mouth, I start to question myself again.

Maybe there is something between them.

Argh! This is so frustrating. I wish I could have a clear-cut sign that Roxy is a total bitch or she's not half bad. Which is it? Did she take those photos of Layla or not? Does she actually like Tyler, or is it all an act to piss me off?

Accelerating with my foot, I head to the park, my insides growing with agitation as I'm tormented by images of Roxy in Tyler's arms, worry over who took those damn photos, and then dread for arriving home to a zealous mother no doubt laden with a selection of clothes I'd rather shred than wear.

I arrive at the park fifteen minutes later. Stopping on the edge of the grass, I flick my board up and have to smile as I watch the chaotic game. Mack has his arms around Kaija's waist and he's spinning her around, her legs lifting like helicopter blades as she laughs and tips her head back against his shoulder. They tumble to the ground while Tori scoots past them, right into the end zone. Her curls go crazy as she jumps up and down. Her laughter turns into a scream as Colt picks her up and throws her over his shoulder.

"No touch down!" he yells.

"No fair!" all the girls yell back.

Finn starts laughing. "That's not the end zone!"

"Yes, it is!" Layla shouts.

Mack shakes his head. "No way. It's down by my book bag."

"Get real!" Kaija stands up, crossing her arms and shooting him a playful glare. "Can't believe you guys have to cheat to beat a bunch of chicks."

"Cheat? We gave you Flash!"

Tyler throws his muscled arms wide, putting on that cocky grin I love. "And that's all you need, baby."

Mack rolls his eyes with a groan while Kaija laughs and extends her hand to help him up. He takes it and pulls her against him as soon as they're standing.

I hate that my stomach goes mushy watching them kiss, but it does…because it reminds me of Tyler's kiss. The way Mack's touching her face, that *lost in it* vibe they're giving off.

A football to Mack's butt puts a quick end to their PDA session. Tyler laughs and starts sprinting away when Mack gives chase. There's no way in hell Mack's going to catch him, but he doesn't give up until Tyler turns and starts sprinting past me.

He jerks to a stop when he notices me, his lips wobbling as if they can't decide whether to smile or frown. I never get a chance to find out because Mack tackles him from behind and they flop to the ground together.

"Hey, Sammy." Mack grins up at me while Tyler wrestles out from beneath him. "Wanna play?"

Tyler answers for me. "No, man, she can't."

He should know better.

For one, I hate it when people answer for me, and even more than that, I hate it when people tell me I can't do something. Especially some jerk who likes to make out with my sister.

Laying my skateboard down, I ignore the fact my arm is in a cast and say, "Sure, I'm in."

The irritated look Tyler throws me only fuels my determination. Ripping my sling off, I dump it by my board and stalk past him, walking over to Finn while Mack organizes everyone into new teams.

19

MESSED-UP BRAIN

TYLER

"HEADS UP!" I throw the football to Mack, having to call for his attention or he'll get hit in the head. We formed new teams only twenty minutes ago and I'm already over it. Of course Mack put himself with Kaija, but come on, does he have to kiss her in every frickin' huddle?

Don't get me wrong. I'm happy for Mack, and I think it's awesome that Kiwi Girl had the guts to come back after everything that went down. But those two are obsessed with each other. Between them, Colt and Tori, and Layla and Finn, the whole couples thing is getting kind of old.

I ignore the little voice in the back of my head telling

me I'm full of shit and that's not what's really bothering me.

Sammy jogs back to my side and gets in position next to me.

"You sure you should be playing?" I ask for about the tenth time.

She growls over her shoulder. "Would you shut up already? I'm fine."

"Your arm should be in a sling."

"I'll put it on after the game." She gives me a pointed look and I know it'll be a waste of time competing with it.

Instead, I look across to Mack's team and give each of the guys a warning glare. I've already told them to take it easy on Sam and they've promised me they will, but I'm going to keep reminding them before every single play.

I crouch down and get ready for Tori to call the play. It's kind of funny watching her hover above Colt as he crouches low, ready to feed her the ball. She's going to hand it off to Kaija, who will make a run for our end zone.

Not happening.

"Hut, hut!" Tori shouts and I surge forward, already marking Kaija.

Mack shoots sideways to block for her but I spin around him and take off down the field, racing after the kiwi girl. Shit, she's fast. I put on an extra burst of speed and touch her back, but not quite fast enough.

Her team makes the down and we reset play a little closer to our end zone.

I'm not usually an ultra-competitive guy unless we're playing a real game in uniform, but I'm hungry for a win today. Maybe it's this other crap that's digging around in the back of my brain. I'm not sure, but losing is going to put me in a really bad mood. I can already feel it brewing.

Finn grins at me as we get into our positions. "Nice run."

"We have to nail them on this down, man. I want that ball back."

Finn laughs, then checks on Layla before getting ready to chase after Tori. She sets up behind Colt again and yells, "Hut, hut!"

This time, she runs back and sets for the pass. Colt shoots forward to catch, but Sammy breaks to the side and intercepts the ball before he can reach it. They knock into each other and flop to the ground, Sammy hugging the ball like a teddy bear.

"Sammy!" I lurch in her direction.

I drop to my knees beside her, pushing the hair out of her face so I can read her expression. There's a slight tightening around the corners of her eyes and I can tell the fall hurt her.

"That's it. You're not playing anymore."

"Would you stop? I'm fine!" She thumps the ball into my stomach and grabs Colt's outstretched hand. He hauls her to her feet and pats her shoulder.

"Nice play, Sam."

"Thanks," she mumbles, rubbing her arm and slowly walking over to Finn.

I stalk across to our huddle and lean in, glaring at Sam before turning to Finn for instructions.

"What do you guys think? An easy pass to Tyler on the outside?"

Layla shrugs. "Whatever. I may have been standing on the sidelines for like three years waving my pompoms for you guys, but I still don't really know what I'm doing."

Finn gives her an adoring smile before kissing her forehead. I roll my eyes. We're in the middle of a football game, for crying out loud! Leave the smooching for later.

I bite back my sharp thoughts and catch Finn's eye. "I don't care what the play is, as long as Sam stays out of harm's way."

A sharp backhand slap to my shoulder makes me stand tall. I scowl at Sammy, rubbing the sore spot she left behind.

"Would you stop treating me like a piece of china? What is your problem today?"

"My problem is that you have a *broken* wrist! You shouldn't be playing!"

"Oh, great, so I just have to stop living until my cast is off?"

"That's not what I'm saying, Sammy."

"Then what *are* you saying?"

"I don't want to see you get hurt again!" I bellow in her face.

My loud confession makes her jerk back. Her forehead wrinkles with a frown and she looks to the grass under our feet. I'm not loving this tension between us, and I hate that I can't fix it. Sammy's always been my man, but now she's not. Now she's the girl who got hurt, the girl I kissed, and now I have the overwhelming urge to both avoid her and protect her.

It's so messed up.

A car horn beeps behind me and I spin to see who it is. Anything to avoid the awkward tension in our huddle. Roxy gets out of the driver's side and waves her fingers at me.

I should be excited to see her, racing across the field like an excited puppy, but I'm no Mack...and she's no Kaija.

Clearing my throat, I drop the ball and amble across the grass. Her smile is all sexy as she wanders around the car to me.

"Hey." She breathes out the word. I'm expecting it to send that tingle running down my spine, but it doesn't.

Pulling my lips into a smile, I stop just in front of her. "Hey, Foxy Roxy. Come to play a little ball?"

She sniggers. "As if. No, I've come to collect Layla. We're going to do a few last-minute things before prom." Her eyebrows wiggle, reminding me of Sammy and the day we talked about sex.

I swallow, trying to force the thought from my mind. Stepping a little closer, I place my hand on her hip. It feels weird acting like her boyfriend. I mean, I'm not. At least I don't think I am. I'm just her date for prom...

the guy she makes out with when she feels like it. Those kisses are always initiated by her, though. She flinches at my touch but doesn't shift away when I lean in close. Her eyes dart over my shoulder and then her lips curl with a cat-like smile as I press my lips against hers.

I'm not sure why I'm starting some hot kiss right now.

Is it a test?

Am I trying to figure out if the Sammy kiss has ruined everything for me?

Or am I actually after what all my friends have—a girl who makes me want to kiss her every chance I get?

Roxy responds to my touch, leaning into it, running her fingers through my hair and swiping her tongue inside my mouth. I kiss her hard, closing my eyes and trying to dive into that *nothing else exists* moment, but I can still hear the murmurs of my friends behind me. I can still feel their eyes on my back.

Gripping Roxy's hip, I try a little harder, but it doesn't work.

I may be kissing the hottest chick at Nelson High right now, but she's not enough to block out the world.

20

NAME RECOGNITION

SAMMY

I TAKE a swig of water then drop the bottle at my feet. Tyler and Roxy are making out by her car.

I feel sick.

Reaching for my sling, I slide it over my head and settle my aching arm back into the material. Like I'm ever going to admit how much smacking into Colt hurt. I wasn't about to be treated like some porcelain doll by a guy who is currently sucking face with my sister.

I didn't know how to respond when he said he didn't want to see me get hurt again. There was something in his desperate tone that jolted me. Like somehow my pain caused him pain. I don't know. Whatever. He's making out with Roxy.

"Are you sure you don't want to come to prom with us?" Tori perches on the edge of the table, hugging the football against her chest. "I really want you to be there."

"Me too." Kaija rests her hip against the edge. "It's not like you need a date. We'll all go as a big group."

"Yeah, and then when some sappy love song comes on, you'll all stare at each other with dreamy eyes and start playing tonsil hockey while I stand on the edge of the room trying not to gag."

Kaija laughs.

"Seriously, guys." I wave my hand at them. "It's not my thing. I'm not even interested in going."

"Not even a little bit?" Tori's nose wrinkles as she holds her fingers a quarter of an inch apart.

I shake my head at her. It's impossible not to smile when she's pulling that adorable face. I'm not giving into those pleading eyes, though. I'd rather slit my wrists than spend the night watching Roxy and Tyler make out.

I glance down to the curb. Yep, they're still at it.

Clenching my jaw, I turn away and hope like hell Roxy means it. I mean, I actually don't want her to mean it at all, but I also don't want Tyler to get hurt.

Huh.

Maybe I do understand how he feels about the whole pain causes pain thing. Seeing him cut up over Roxy would injure me big time. Tyler might act like a cocky shit sometimes, but he's a good guy...a *really* good guy, and he deserves to be treated like one.

If Roxy's planning on dumping Tyler straight after prom...

I shake my head, picturing the scene and his crestfallen face.

But what can I do?

Pursing my lips, I stare across the grass, studying the way Roxy's fingers pinch Tyler's neck, noting the light hold he has on her hip. Their kiss is getting kind of robotic, actually. They don't have that natural connection that everyone else around me seems to have.

Kaija nudges my arm. "You okay?"

I blink and force myself to look at her.

Her green eyes sparkle with a look that sees right through me. My eyebrows dip and I gaze down at my worn Converse.

"You don't like your sister dating your mate?"

I shrug and lead in with a lie. "I don't care. Just as long as she means it," I mutter.

"Ah, I see. You're worried she's stringing him along."

"I would be," Tori mumbles, then gives me a sheepish look. "Sorry, no offense to your sister or anything. I just…find it hard to trust her."

I tip my head with a raised eyebrow, letting Tori off. Roxy's never given Pixie Girl any reason to think otherwise.

"I'm sure Tyler knows what he's getting into. He doesn't seem like the fall-hard kind of guy anyway." Kaija pats my arm.

"Yeah, but he seems kind of into Roxy right now," I murmur.

Tori squeezes my uninjured wrist, giving me a kind smile. She doesn't have to say anything, but I can tell what she's thinking—*it's not fair. Tyler should be with you.*

I'm grateful for her sweet sentiment, but it still doesn't change the fact that Tyler's making out with Roxy.

Cradling my aching arm, I glance across to my sister, telling myself it has to be the last time I do it.

They're just pulling out of the kiss and now they're hugging. I catch Roxy's gaze over Tyler's shoulder and she gives me this little smirk, her blue eyes gleaming.

Kaija scoffs. "She reminds me so much of Anna sometimes. Such a dick tease."

"Anna?" The name sparks something in my brain. I'm scrambling to place it.

"Yeah." Kaija sighs. "We used to be best friends until she totally dumped me in it, blaming me entirely for what went down." She bites the edge of her lip. "You know, the cartoon thing."

I nod. Mack filled me in when he was trying to get me to sneak into Dana's place and look for evidence against Anderson Foster.

"Anyway, she and my ex-boyfriend completely turned on me and made everything a million times worse."

"What's his name?"

"Huh?" Kaija looks up at me.

"Your ex-boyfriend. What's his name?"

"Oh, Hanson." She pokes out her tongue in disgust.

Click! And there it is. Those diary pages. The ones on Roxy's camera. Anna and HANSON written in capital letters with lots of exclamation marks. I can't breathe for a second as I figure out that those pages must be photos of letters…and they must be about Kaija.

The hideous cartoon of Kaija's shame flashes through my mind, the whole story laid bare in stick-figure detail.

Kiwi Girl's still talking, but I'm only just registering her words. "He's like the coolest guy in my school."

"And the world's biggest assbutt." Mack pulls me back into the conversation, sidling up behind Kaija and gliding his arm around her waist.

Kaija smiles up at him and he takes the opportunity to kiss her nose. I can do nothing but stare at them as my mind is once again overrun with images of scribbled writing and the big, fat question: What were they doing on Roxy's camera?

I think I know.

In fact, I *know* I know.

So that leaves me with another question that will no doubt eat me alive. Should I really be waiting until *after* prom to bring this all to light?

If I care about Tyler, shouldn't I be doing everything in my power to protect him from the Roxanator?

21

ICY-BLUE VENEER

TYLER

ROXY STEPS OUT of my embrace and gives me one more flirty smile before turning to Layla, who is now hovering next to us.

"You ready to go?" she asks.

Roxy nods and turns to me with her sexy grin. "See you later, stud."

She winks and I grin and wave her off.

My smile loses power the second she pulls away. Kissing Roxy is hot, I can't deny it, but it still doesn't hold a candle to Sammy. That hospital kiss was something different. I'd never relived a kiss so much in my life, and it bothers me that Roxy's hot lips can't wipe it from my mind.

I'm supposed to be taking Queen Roxy to prom, becoming king for a night and setting myself up for an awesome senior year.

I look over my shoulder at the group of friends I'm gonna miss so badly. They're standing around, relaxed and happy.

All except Sammy. She's got this weird look on her face. She's staring into the distance, acting like she's not hearing anything that's being said.

I don't know what it's about and I'm curious, but I don't want to get into another fight. Sammy riled is usually fun, but that's because she's never riled at me. Usually, it's the two of us fighting side-by-side, not face-to-face.

I hate this.

My surefire plans for greatness are feeling shaky and it's all because I crossed a line with my best friend and ruined everything.

Shoving my hands in my pockets, I wander back over to the group, trying to act casual and happy. Not wanting to disrupt the vibe.

"How's Roxy doing?" Colt waggles his eyebrows at me.

I snicker. "Yeah, good. She told me what she's wearing to prom. Sounds pretty freaking hot to me."

"Nice." Colt nods.

"Yeah, it's some kind of pink dress."

Sammy rolls her eyes. "Big surprise."

I ignore her dry tone and look to Tori and Kaija. They're girls. They should know this stuff. "So, I've rented a black suit. Do you think I should go for like a pink tie, or—?"

"Not go at all!" Sammy snaps.

I turn to look at her. "What?"

"Oh, come on, Ty." She flicks her hands up. "She doesn't want to go with you. She's doing it to cause trouble."

Her words, the way she's firing them at me—it's kind of hard not to be offended. What the hell is she trying to say? That I'm not good enough for Roxy? That the thought of us going together is just some big joke?

I should just mumble *whatever* and walk away, but for some reason, I can't let this go. "How is going with me causing trouble?"

Sammy points across to Mack-Attack, casting me in a big, fat shadow. "Everyone knows she wanted to go with Mack, but he refused her and now the girl who has taken her place arrives out of the blue to ruin everything."

195

Kaija's head snaps back and she frowns at Mack, who just shakes his head. "She asked but I said no."

"Which really pissed her off, but she's not about to admit that to anybody, right? So what does she do? She goes after the one guy who—" Sammy looks down and swallows.

"Who what?" I bark.

Shaking her head, she shoves her hand in her pocket and looks to the ground. Her long hair flops off her shoulder, hiding her face from me.

"What, Sammy?"

"She's settling for you." She sighs. "Don't you get it? She doesn't want to go to prom on her own! Mack and Colt are both taken. Finn's now with her best friend so she goes for..." Sammy points her finger at me, fueling my insecurity and pissing me off.

Well, this is a news flash. Here I was thinking Roxy liked me, like maybe I was good enough after all. Her kisses certainly indicated that she didn't mind me! Gritting my teeth, I throw Sammy a warning glare to shut the hell up. If she keeps ranting like this, she might end up making some derogatory comment about the secret I told her.

I jump in before she can do any damage. "You're just jealous because no one's asked you."

She flinches at my sharp tone, then glares up at me. "As if I would even want to go!"

Her eyes flash, showing me a glimpse of something painful. Shit, no one did ask her. I was going to try and hook up with Darius or Will to take her, but I forgot… or maybe I hated the idea of her going with another guy. Geez, I'm an asshole sometimes. Whatever my reasons, it doesn't change the fact that this weekend I'm heading to prom with all my friends and Sammy's gonna be left behind.

In typical Sammy style, she tucks her emotions away behind an icy-blue veneer, not letting anyone see how crappy she must be feeling.

I swallow, regret scraping my spine like sharp talons. "You know you could still come—"

She cuts off my peace offering by grabbing my shirt collar and making everything worse. "You listen to me, you dumb shit. My sister likes to stir things up, so watch your frickin' back on Saturday night." She shoves me away from her. "It wouldn't shock me if you find a knife buried between your shoulder blades before the end of the evening."

Her lack of faith in me turns my peace offering to a pile of ash. The idea that Roxy is just using me is a punch in the gut, shattering all illusions that I'm even worthy of taking the hot cheerleader. I don't want Sammy to come if she's going to be waiting around for my humiliating downfall.

It's so unlike her to act this way. I should be asking her why she's even thinking this shit, but I'm too hurt and riled.

So, like the true idiot I am, I deal with her warning the only way I know how—with a snarky little comeback that hides how much she's wounding me.

"Thanks, Sams." I flip her off. "It's nice to know you think so much of me."

She lifts her middle finger right back at me. "Yeah, well, that's what friends are for, right?" She shoves past me, ensuring her left shoulder clips me on the way. I take a step back but keep staring straight ahead, refusing to watch her stalk off.

Her skateboard smacks onto the ground and I listen to the wheels on the concrete as she rolls away from us. She shouldn't be boarding with a broken wrist and I nearly yell that out, but I'm too pissed to speak.

The silence that follows is way awkward. I'm not about to fill it; I'm too humiliated. Sammy and I have had our scraps in the past, but this one feels different, more intense and destructive.

Finn eventually clears his throat. "Do you think she

was serious…about Roxy causing trouble?" His brown eyes flicker with worry.

"Nah." I brush my hand through the air. "She's just mad at me for taking her sister. You know how much those two hate each other."

Mack wraps his arm around Kaija's shoulder and kisses the side of her head, concern flickering over his expression.

Kaija squeezes his forearm. "Hey, I didn't fly all the way over to my one and only prom just to have some cheerleader ruin it for me." Looking at me with a wink and a smile, she says, "Don't worry about it, Tyler. I can handle a little Roxanne Carmichael."

I snicker, hoping she doesn't have to handle anything.

Shit, Sammy better not be right.

Forcing a nod, I look around at my friends. "Yeah, it's gonna be a good night."

"The best," Tori agrees quietly.

Funny how it looks like none of us really believe her.

22

THE TRUTH SUCKS

SAMMY

I'M such an idiot for going off on Tyler like that. I shouldn't have said anything. Making an impulse decision to do big things is always stupid. All I did was piss him off and make things super awkward for everyone.

Stalking out of the cafeteria, I let the doors shut behind me, trying to rid myself of the nonchalant look Tyler shot me when I walked past his table. Brushing things off is always his first line of defense. If things get uncomfortable, he tends to walk away. I crossed a line yesterday afternoon, getting in his face like that, and now I'm paying for it.

Shit, I hope I haven't lost him.

This sucks.

I hate feeling this desperate for a guy who's always been there. I want to go back to what we had. I wish we'd never kissed. I wish Roxy had never seen me drooling over him that day.

Roxy. The word tastes bitter in my mouth. I couldn't sleep last night thanks to her and the massive argument over trying to borrow one of her outfits. For once, Mom tried to be my advocate, but of course ended up smoothing things over by offering to buy Roxy a little something new as a reward for letting me borrow this ugly purple shirt she found for me. I walked out of the house with a fake smile, normal clothes tucked safely inside my bag. I'd have to remember to change again before I got home.

Making a fist, I have to seriously resist the urge to punch the bright pink prom queen poster on the wall. Damn Roxy with her stupid wink and irritating slogans! I hate how perfect she always looks. The smile people get on their faces when they see her coming. That dopey look in their eyes, like she's some freaking celebrity.

She's not!

But it's kind of hard to counter that belief when everyone around her makes her feel that way...even Mom!

A shudder jerks my spine as I relive the torture of my

mother's fussing this morning. That proud look on her face as I shuffled out the door pretending that I wanted to be more like my sister. That's not me! I don't do that kind of shit!

My mind's just messed up right now. Wading through this Tyler/Roxy nightmare is making me stupid.

If I'm not obsessing over the photos on her camera, I'm reliving images of her and Tyler making out—over and over again.

Rubbing my eyes, I flick the hair out of my face and veer left. The bell isn't due to ring for another ten minutes, so I'm just aimlessly stalking the halls while I try to walk out my problems.

The more I think about it, the more I'm convinced that those pages of text on Roxy's camera were diary entries. It makes sense that it'd be Kaija's diary, right? I mean, her friends' names were mentioned all through it. That must have been how Roxy found out about her little (kind of gigantic) secret. So, how did Roxy get access to those pages?

I screech to a stop and whisper, "Dana Foster."

Our cute little next-door neighbor.

Kaija lived with the Fosters while she was here, which meant Dana would have had access to her bedroom.

That's why she's been acting so weird around Roxy lately. She knows something.

Taking a right, I run down the corridor, hoping to catch the freshman before the bell rings. I don't really know where she'll be, but there are a few places I can try. I've got a pretty good scope of this school and the student cliques. It's the beauty of being a nomad.

Heading for the small outside quad near the art department, I cross my fingers that she'll be loitering nearby...and for once, I get lucky.

Like really lucky.

I don't even make it to the quad before I spot her scuttling along the edge of the hallway. Her wide brown curls bounce around her face as she takes these short quick steps.

I move to the side and block her.

She jerks to a stop with a little gasp and looks up at me.

"We need to talk."

The second the words come out of my mouth her eyes bulge and her face drains of color. Like seriously, I'm watching her go pale.

"Um." She bites her lips together. "I'm kind of busy right now..."

"Yeah, with me." I tuck my left hand under her arm and drag her to the girls' bathroom. Closing the door behind us, I check the stalls to make sure we're alone before leaning against the main doorway to make sure we aren't interrupted.

Dana wrings her hands and starts nibbling her lip so hard I think it's about to bleed.

"Tell me why Roxy has pictures of Kaija's diary on her camera."

Dana's large eyes pop up and stare right at me. "She showed you?"

"No, I accidentally found them. How did they get there?"

The toilet in the end stall is running. It must be jammed. That along with the dripping tap in the sink closest to Dana suddenly makes this feel like some kind of Nazi interrogation.

Seriously, I need to stop doing my world history homework.

"Dana, come on! What happened?"

"She made me promise not to tell," Dana whispers, genuine fear flashing in her eyes.

I sigh and force my voice to a soft lilt. "I'm not going to

let anything bad happen to you. But I need to know the truth. What has my sister been up to?"

Dana's swallow is audible as she rubs her thumb into the palm of her hand. "It was after New Year's Eve. My family took Kaija away for the weekend, but I had to stay behind to finish my homework. Roxy showed up, which was so surprising. She never talks to me, but she was being so nice and I've wanted to be part of that crowd for so long." Her cheeks tinge red. "I would've done anything to get in good with her, so when she told me she needed to see Kaija's bedroom, I invited her in without even thinking about it. I asked her what she was looking for and she told me that Kaija had done something that made her suspicious. She didn't say anything else, just that she needed to keep her friends safe."

My eyes narrow and Dana shakes her head.

"I know it was stupid, okay? I should have asked more questions! You don't have to glare at me like that. I've been beating myself up for weeks!"

I sigh and look to the floor so I'm not tempted to scowl at her again. I can't believe she just let Roxy go through Kaija's bedroom!

Dana pulls in a ragged breath and keeps going. "I swear I didn't know what she had planned. I thought she was just going to have a quick look around Kaija's bedroom, but she really started hunting, going through Kaija's drawers and stuff. Nothing popped, but then I… I found Kaija's diary hidden under the mattress. Roxy was so pleased with me and the more she sat there reading, the happier she got. She even invited me to sit with her at lunch when school got back. I was too stoked to think past what she might do. She came back about twenty minutes later with her camera and took a bunch of photos, then used my computer to hunt for some girl on Facebook."

Thumping my head lightly against the bathroom door, I close my eyes, nausea rolling through me. "Was it Anna?"

"I'm not sure, but she ended up finding some stick-figure cartoon drawings…" Dana's voice peters off. "I didn't know they were of Kaija until I got to school on Monday morning and saw the whole story. I had no idea Roxy would post them everywhere, and at first I thought it was just a joke. But the way Kaija reacted…" Scratching the side of her nose, Dana sniffs. "Roxy found me later that day to ask me what I thought of the drawings. I was too afraid to say anything, so she just smiled at me and told me that she never realized how much fun art could be and that if I ever wanted her to draw pictures of me, she'd be happy to." Dana closes her eyes and two tears escape, one down each cheek. "It won't matter if the story's truth or fiction. Roxy can annihilate me. She can take down anyone."

Stepping forward, I squeeze Dana's shoulder and try to give her my kindest smile. "I'm not going to let her do that."

"Please don't tell her I told you."

"I won't." I look her in the eye. "I promise."

"I never meant to hurt Kaija that way. I was just so caught up in wanting to be…cool."

"Cool's way over-rated. Trust me."

She snickers and wipes the tears off her face.

The bathroom door pops open. I sidestep to cover Dana from view, then put on a breezy tone. "Catch ya later, neighbor."

"S-see ya," Dana calls after me as I slip out the door.

I don't know who just walked in, but hopefully Dana can put on a bright smile. That conversation we just had needs to stay as covert as possible…until I'm ready to blow the lid on this thing.

I really want to find Tyler and give him the lowdown, but I doubt he'll be up for it today. Prom's tomorrow night and I don't trust Roxy not to do something evil to him if he doesn't pick her up on time and be the date she wants him to be.

Shit, this is bad.

My own sister.

I mean, I knew she had it in her, but I never thought she'd actually go through with it. Those cartoons were a true testament to her malice and just one more piece of proof that she knows all about those pictures of Derek, Quaid, and Layla.

A shudder races down my spine as I picture that final photo again…the one that's eating me alive.

23

EVERY CHOICE HAS CONSEQUENCES

TYLER

MY INSIDES ARE RATTLING as I walk up the path to Roxy's front door. I'm decked out in my suit and hot pink tie, looking pretty damn fine. I'm not going to admit this to anyone, but I seriously took my time getting ready. Shiloh was pounding on the bathroom door by the time I was done.

"Really?" She crossed her arms with a skeptical glare when I finally opened the door. "I waited that long for this?"

I tweaked her nose and then tickled her until she admitted how handsome I looked. Braxton jumped on my back, always up for a play fight. Thankfully, Mom stepped in to rescue me before my suit got messed up.

"You look gorgeous. Roxy's going to swoon when she sees you."

Adjusting my tie with a nervous smile, I knock on the door and hope Mom's right.

Sammy answers. Her blue eyes bulge for a split second, her eyes racing down my body before she swallows and pulls her expression into line.

She gives me that standard *bored* look of hers and mutters, "She's not ready yet."

Moving away from the door, she leaves it open for me and stalks into the living room.

My gut twists, killing off the nervous rattles and making me feel like shit again. I never should have spoken to her the way I did at the park. I was just pissed that she was getting in my face and making me feel like a pathetic nobody that Roxy is just going to use and discard like a piece of trash.

Sammy and I hardly ever fight. The odd bicker, nothing nasty. But her words hurt and so I bit back...and achieved nothing.

Stepping into the house, I gently shut the door behind me and follow my friend. She's slumped on the couch with her legs crossed playing *Star Wars Battlefront*. I love that game. Over spring break, Sammy and I spent a few hours each night killing at it. Part of me wants to sit down and join her. A much bigger part than I counted on.

I shuffle over to the couch and take a seat, watching the TV as storm troopers attack from the left.

I point at the screen. "Watch your ten."

"Got it." She blasts them down and keeps moving through the battle station.

"Is this multiplayer?"

"Nah, just...solo." The way she whispers the word 'solo' hits me right in the chest, like she's talking about way more than the game.

My suit jacket rustles as I turn to face her. She keeps her eyes focused on the screen, but I can tell she knows I'm looking. Her jaw is tense, her forehead wrinkling as she tries to concentrate.

"Does it hurt to play with your broken wrist?"

She shakes her head, but it's obvious she's lying.

With a sigh, I place my hand over the remote and gently take it out of her hands.

"Hey!"

"We need to talk."

"No, I need to play." She grabs for the remote, but I hold it out of her way.

Her thunderous look is kind of adorable and I snicker.

Bad move.

Her eyes narrow to tiny slits and she lunges for the remote. I pull my arm back and she flops into my lap. I catch her waist before she rolls onto the floor and gaze down at those blue eyes...hypnotized.

I don't actually know what's happening right now. All I can do is stare at her and just breathe. Her face is inches from mine. One little move forward and I could be kissing her again.

Does she want me to?

Her eyes are kind of saying that she does, but...it's Sammy.

I mean, she's like one of my bros.

A very kissable one.

My tongue sweeps across my bottom lip and I'm thinking about our hospital kiss so hard right now. If she doesn't move, I won't be able to resist.

"She's nearly ready!" Mrs. Carmichael calls from upstairs, shocking Sammy off my lap. She thuds onto the floor and scrambles away from me, taking a seat on the other side of the room.

Running her left hand through her fine hair, she

bunches it at the nape of her neck and stares at the floor. I hate this. I miss our easy banter, the way I could tell her anything and not have to think twice about the words coming out of my mouth.

"I'm sorry," I mumble, squeezing my knuckles and wincing. "I shouldn't have yelled at you at the park. I should've been inviting you to prom, hooking you up with a date."

She scoffs and shakes her head.

"I'm serious, Sam."

"I don't need you to find me a date." Her blue eyes hit me again, like laser beams to the forehead. "I wouldn't go, even if some guy was stupid enough to ask me. I'm not prom material, Ty. Can you honestly imagine me in a dress?"

I can't help a snicker as comical images of Sammy decked out in finery race through my mind.

She rolls her eyes and looks to the ceiling. "You're taking the girl you wanted to…and you're going to look great together."

Her smile is crooked and weak when she glances across at me.

Something's happening to her eyes. I've never seen them so shiny before. Shit, is she about to cry?

It feels like a puncture wound. I tear my eyes away from that face, scared my whole world's about to shatter. Samantha Carmichael is the toughest chick I know. She doesn't cry about anything…but she looks like she's about to cry over me. What does that even mean?

I glance back up to see her bite her lips together and let her hair go. The long locks drape over her shoulders, hiding her face in shadow. With a quick sniff, she runs her finger under her nose and stands up.

Noises on the stairwell make me jerk out of my seat. The nerves are back, hammering at me from all sides. It only gets worse when Roxy appears looking so many kinds of hot I can't breathe for a second.

Her blue eyes are made vibrant by perfect makeup. Her full, kissable lips smile at me when she dips her hip to show off the stunning pink dress. It's one of those floaty ones that goes all the way to the floor, but the top part is cool, with these sparkly diamond things that cover the strapless, fitted bodice. I can see the top of her boobs and my mouth waters of its own accord.

Damn. She is fine.

"Wow." It's all I can manage.

Roxy's pink lips pull into a sexy smirk, like she already knows how great she looks. I step toward her and she glances over my shoulder, her eyes gleaming before she grabs the back of my neck and pulls me in for a kiss.

It's kind of awkward considering her mom is standing right there, plus my mind can't get away from Sammy.

I pull out of the kiss and smile at Roxy, reminding myself that I'm getting exactly what I wanted. I'm taking the hottest chick in Nelson High to the prom.

So why doesn't it feel better?

"Photo time!" Mrs. Carmichael sings as she holds up a small, silver camera.

I nestle my arm around Roxy's waist and she leans into me, putting on the perfect pose. Her mother grins and lifts the camera. "So beautiful."

Forcing my best smile, I hold it in place while Mrs. Carmichael goes a little camera happy. Click-click-click.

"You're going to run out of memory," Sammy mutters from the living room.

"Just one more," her mother chirps. "It's not every day your baby girl goes to prom looking so beautiful."

Sammy rolls her eyes. "Aren't they going to some professional shoot on the way? Why do you need more photos?"

"Photos are memories, Samantha," her mom chides, snapping another picture before turning to me with a tight smile.

"Yeah, don't be jealous, sis." Roxy's voice is sickly

sweet. "It's your choice to act like a she-man. And we all know that every choice…"

"Has consequences," Roxy and her mother finish in unison.

Sammy replies with a dry glare, hot enough to melt steel. Roxy leans against me with a little giggle, and I can't help feeling sorry for my friend. With her dad away so much, she's kind of outnumbered in this place. Do they have any idea how much they're humiliating her right now? And how much more I think of her for responding so calmly?

Roxy shakes my lapel, grabbing my attention. I glance down at her beaming smile.

"Let's go, handsome." She winks. "We're picking up Michelle and her date on the way to the lake. I've scoped out the perfect place to get the best shots of us. The photographer should be waiting there already."

"You girls are going to look so amazing," her mom practically sings. "A trio of beauties. Can't wait to see the photos."

"Oh, it's just me and Michelle this year, Mom." Roxy's lips pinch tight.

"Where will Layla be?"

"Busy with her boyfriend." Roxy takes my hand, her fingers squeezing me tightly. "We'll see them at prom."

I force a closed-mouth grin and try to hide my surprise. I had no idea my buddies weren't going to be there for the photoshoot. I only found out about the professional photographer a couple of days ago. Roxy planned it all and I just assumed she'd include everybody.

Obviously not.

"Have a good night, you two." Mrs. Carmichael pats my shoulder excitedly before adjusting one of Roxy's loose curls. "You look so beautiful."

Her eyes are brimming with pride.

"I'll have her home by—"

"Oh, don't you worry about that. I just want you to have the best night of your lives. Can't wait to see that crown, baby girl."

Roxy glides out the door, calling over her shoulder, "Thanks, Mom."

I follow after her but then rush ahead to open the limo door.

"Thank you," she purrs before gliding inside.

I should be the happiest guy in the world tonight, but I'm struggling to find that giddy sensation. Glancing back at the house, I gaze at the darkened living room window and wonder for a second what it'd be like to jump into the limo with Sammy.

Fun.

That three-letter word sums up Sammy perfectly.

Pushing the thought aside, I take my seat next to Roxy, giving her another closed-mouth grin before telling the driver where Michelle lives.

24

TREEHOUSE CRY-FEST

SAMMY

I STARE OUT THE WINDOW, hoping I'm invisible as I watch Tyler open the door for Roxy. They do look good together. Mom was right to take a gazillion photos.

Photos.

Ugh.

I hate this.

Screw Tyler's big night. I should have just told him the truth before he flounced out of the house with my sexy sister. Is she going to coax him into doing it tonight?

I can't think about it.

Tyler turns around to look at the house. I duck into the shadows and close my eyes, counting to fifty before slowly spinning back to watch the limo pulling out of our driveway.

"Samantha?" Mom pops into the living room. "What are you doing, sweetie?"

"Nothing," I mutter, moving away from the curtain and grabbing the PlayStation remote.

"Should you really be playing that with your broken wrist?"

I plunk onto the couch and scowl at her. "What else am I supposed to do?"

Mom crosses her arms and leans against the arch frame. "You should be going to prom with your sister."

"News flash, Mom: I wasn't invited."

"Did you even try? I mean, surely there's someone you could have gone with… a group of friends? That guy you like? Did you even ask him?"

I shake my head. "Everyone already had a date. And I don't even want to go." I make a face, sticking my tongue out like I've just drunk a glass of sour lemon juice.

Mom sighs and walks into the room, taking a seat beside me.

Groan! Here we go.

"Sweetie." Mom runs her hand down my arm. "It's not healthy for you to separate yourself from the crowd. You need to form solid friendships. It enriches your life. Now, I'm not blind. I know you and Roxanne aren't the best of friends, which is why it's so important that you reach out to others. You have to try. You can't just expect things to fall into your lap. I know it takes effort to put yourself out there, but—"

"I did try!" I shut her up, slapping the controller down. "I'm not... He's never going to see me that way, alright? What's the point of torturing myself?"

"Well, you showed some promise the other day, trying to find a new look. Boys appreciate that. Maybe we can work this out together." Mom tucks a lock of hair behind my ear. "You could be really pretty, if you just..."

My head jerks to face her. "Have a makeover? Change myself? Become someone different?"

"Samantha, I'm just..."

"No!" I lurch off the couch. "Just forget it! You've got your pretty little daughter, and I'm sorry that I can't give you two. I just want to be me, and I want that to be okay. I want it to be enough!"

I don't give Mom a chance to reply. Spinning around, I stalk to the door, shoving my feet into my ripped Vans before tearing out of the house. I don't know where I'm going yet, but I'm sure I'll figure it out. I just want to get away from pretty people with their stupid makeup, sweet-smelling perfumes, and ridiculous expectations.

Sprinting down the street, I ignore the pounding in my arm and keep going. After about twenty minutes of crazy running, I find myself on Tyler's street. Typical. Of course I ran here without thinking about it.

Puffing like a chain-smoker who's just run a marathon, I slow to a stop outside Tyler's house. Axel starts barking the second I step onto the grass. No lights come on in the house so it's safe to say the Schumanns are probably out for dinner.

Perfect. I don't want to talk to anyone anyway.

Unlatching the gate, I slip on to the property and am immediately pounced on by Axel. His large paws hit my shoulders and he gives me a sniff and a sloppy lick on the cheek.

"Okay, okay." I push him off me, not really in the mood for kisses.

Well, not the doggy kind, anyway.

Shit, I seriously thought Tyler was about to kiss me again in my living room. I don't know what came over us. It was like we were being held in place by some magic glue. If Mom hadn't broken the spell, I'd still be staring at him now, lost in those eyes of his, listening to the sound of his breathing, feeling his hard chest against my arm.

A chest I'll never get to press my cheek against because Roxy's cheek will be there. They'll sway together on that dance floor tonight, lost in some magical moment I'll never get to experience.

My eyes glaze with tears. They hit me with a force I've never felt before. My nose starts dribbling and no amount of sniffing will stop the tingles. Racing away from Axel, I climb the rickety ladder up to the treehouse.

Axel starts barking from below, but I ignore his *you forgot me* whines and curl into a ball on the rough tree-house floor. Tears are blinding me now, threatening to spill down my cheeks. I can't even remember the last time I cried. I'm hating it already.

Closing my eyes, I give up and let the first tear pop free. It rolls down my nose, tickling my lips before I lick it away. The saltiness surprises me.

Sucking in a shuddering breath, I let out a small whimper and finally allow myself to just go for it. My stomach shakes, jerking out my first sob. Tucking my hand beneath my cheek, I set the tears free, crying for everything I'll never have with Tyler.

25

SEEING THE LIGHT

TYLER

ROXY and I walk through an archway made from twisted wire covered in fairy lights. The forest effect is unbelievable and it only gets better as we pop into the main gymnasium.

It looks amazing. The prom committee did a stellar job with their *A Night under the Stars* theme. Glittering fairy lights hang from a central point on the ceiling, looking like a massive chandelier. Crescent moons in shiny silver dangle among them. The walls are glowing with a rich blue color, giving the whole space a magical, ethereal quality. The central dance floor is covered with some kind of silvery glitter, and off to the right is a photo booth area with a massive crescent moon you can sit on. Couples and groups are already lined up and posing.

The DJ is set up on the temporary stage and is mixing some pretty sweet beats. I bob my head, my first genuine smile starting to show.

The photoshoot had been kind of punishing, with Michelle and Roxy wanting to look perfect in every shot. It's hard to get into it when you're being bossed around to stand a certain way. It was so fake and plastic and only amplified how much I wished my friends had been there to lighten the mood. The one joke I did crack scored me a scoffing titter and a mild glare. I didn't bother after that and just did what Roxy told me to.

"This place is lit." I laugh, already scanning the area for my friends.

Roxy smiles at me but doesn't say anything. Her hand is in the crook of my arm and I can already feel people checking us out. I get a few impressed smiles from guys on my team…just what I'd been hoping for.

So, again, why doesn't it feel better?

"Hey, Flash!"

I glance up at the sound of my name and spot Finn waving at me. Layla's by his side, looking smoking hot in a vibrant blue dress with silver edging. But the best thing about her is the grin on her face. Her arm's around Finn's waist and she's laughing with Pixie Girl who, hey, doesn't look bad.

Check it out. Pixie Girl's gucci.

Her petite body is wrapped in a bright purple dress that comes to her knees. It's backless but has this gold strap that comes up around her throat. She looks amazing. Colt definitely appreciates it; he can't take his eyes off her.

I steer Roxy in their direction. She's busy talking to Michelle and her date—I don't know, some college guy. I didn't even bother trying to remember his name. I'm only a few feet away when she turns to see where I'm heading.

Jerking my arm, she pulls us to a stop. "Where are you going?"

"To hang out with our friends." I give her a confused frown.

"I didn't come to hang out with them." She smirks. "I came to win a crown and dance with you."

Tugging me away from my buddies, she yanks me onto the dance floor and drapes her arms over my shoulder. I try to focus on how awesome it is that my date is Roxy. People keep glancing at us—girls eyeing up Roxy's stunning dress, guys giving me impressed eyebrow raises behind her back. Resting my hands on her hips, I sway to the beat and try to get into the song, but it's kind of hard when Roxy won't stop looking over my shoulder.

Her full lips are set in this tight line and her eyes keep narrowing at the corners. My forehead wrinkles and I spin her around so I can see who she's eyeing up with such a dark look.

I spot Kaija immediately. She's walking beside Mack, her arm resting on his shoulder as she whispers into his ear. They both smile, oblivious to the ripple effect they always have at this school. Whispers flow through the crowd as everyone steals a glance at them—the celebrity couple. Kaija's in this shimmery gold dress with a plunging neckline and thigh-high split. That thing belongs on the red carpet. Her red platform heels make her the same height as Mack, and she seems to float through the crowd like she's walking on a moving walkway.

Mack tugs her a little closer and kisses her neck. As soon as they reach my friends, Kaija is pulled into a hug by Tori, who has to go up on her tiptoes just to reach Kaija's shoulders. Pixie Girl says something and they all laugh. I bet it was some cute quip about being the midget among them.

I want to be over there. I want to know what she just said.

Tipping my head in their direction, I smile down at Roxy and ask, "You sure you don't want to go hang with Layla?"

The gorgeous brunette makes an ugly face. "She's too busy with Finn…and her new friends."

She glances over her shoulder and then back to me. Damn…if looks could kill.

I frown at Roxy's dark expression. "I thought she was your best friend."

"She is." Roxy rolls her eyes. "But since hooking up with the chocolate wonder, she's seriously changing."

"For the better," I murmur.

"What?" Roxy snaps, pulling away from me. "You think hanging out with the hippy freak and Miss Hobbiton is better? Give me a break, Tyler. I wouldn't have said yes to your invitation if I knew you were going to be spouting this kind of shit. You're like the only normal one left."

Spinning me around, she looks over my shoulder again, her cheekbones protruding as she scowls at my group.

It's weird how I've never really noticed this side of Roxy before. I mean, I knew she could be bitchy, but I always found it kind of a turn-on. I like strong chicks, but nasty? I'm not so sure.

My mood quickly sours as the DJ kicks up a new song and I'm forced to keep dancing with Miss Pouty-Face.

"You're staring," I eventually mutter.

"Excuse me?"

"Didn't your mother ever tell you that was rude?"

She throws me an impatient frown. "What?"

"You're here with me, right?"

"Yes." She says it slowly, like I'm stupid or something.

"So why are you spending the whole time looking over at Mack?"

She opens her mouth to argue, then lets out a little sigh. "Okay, fine, so maybe I'm a little disappointed he wouldn't take me, but I've got you now, so it's all cool."

"But you'd rather have him." My words come out sharp, giving away my mood.

"Don't be like that. Everyone knows Mack and I had a little thing going before *she* showed up and ruined it all." Roxy's fingers dig into my shoulders. "I can't believe she actually had the nerve to come back. I mean, she waltzes into our school cafeteria like she's this innocent flower when it's total bullshit. Those cartoons depicted the truth, you know. She actually drove someone to suicide."

"How'd you know that?"

Roxy's eyes flick to mine. "Do you think she would have run if she hadn't been guilty as sin? And then she has the nerve to show up again and steal my prom king! She's like some virus that just keeps coming back. I don't know what else I'm supposed to do."

I stop dancing, frozen by that one little comment. "What?"

"What!" She pulls me closer and tries to keep swaying, but I don't let her.

Stepping back, I drill her with a look she won't be able to brush off easily. "You just said you don't know what *else* you're supposed to do. What *did* you do?"

Roxy rolls her eyes. "Oh, look, forget it. Let's just ignore her and enjoy our night." Gripping my shoulders, she pulls me back and rises, hoping to plant her lips on mine.

It's not happening.

I dodge the kiss and hold her at arm's length, determined to get the truth. Staring at her irritated expression, I probe in the calmest voice I can.

"Why did you say yes to coming with me?"

She blinks, her eyes round and beautiful. "Because you asked."

"You mean I was stupid enough to think you actually wanted to go with me. That you might actually like me."

"I do like you. Stop talking trash, Tyler."

I shake my head. "You're obsessed with Mack."

She scoffs. "No, I'm not."

"You got rid of Kaija, didn't you? You posted those cartoons." I can't believe I'm accusing her of this. It's dangerous ground I'm walking on here; everybody knows you don't piss off Roxy Carmichael.

She gives me a hard look and I slide my hands into my pockets, not willing to bend. Her right eyebrow arches and she crosses her arms. "Look, I don't know what you're on right now, but cut the shit. This is prom. You seriously want to ruin our night by accusing me of something I didn't do?" She lets out a breath and then puts on a sultry smile, sidling back up against me. "I just want to have fun with you, Tyler. That's why I said yes, because you're the funniest person I know. The biggest goof-ball and the best person at this school to show me a good time."

She runs her finger down my cheek and kisses me. The second her lips brush mine, I think of Sam and am struck by how much I'd rather be hanging out with her.

Skater Girl is the funniest person I know. She's easy to

be around and the best person at this school to show me a good time, so why the hell am I standing on the dance floor making out with her sister?

My eyes ping open and I jerk away from Roxy, wiping my lips with the back of my hand.

Prom is supposed to be a fun night that you celebrate with friends. Like some arrogant idiot, I turned it into a status symbol and missed the whole freaking point.

Glancing over my shoulder, I look for my friends. Finn, Layla, Mack and Kaija are now on the floor, dancing next to each other. They're still talking and laughing and having fun...a fun I should be a part of.

"Tyler, seriously, what is your problem?" Roxy shakes my arm. "Stop embarrassing us and put your arms around me." Her harsh whisper makes me look down at her, and it's like whatever shades were covering my eyes before have been lifted by my revelation. Roxy is beautiful—she always will be—but it's skin deep.

And I guess maybe I'm over being so shallow.

"I gotta go." I move away from her.

"Excuse me?" Her voice pitches high.

"There's somewhere I've gotta be."

Pinching my arm in a vice-like grip, she holds me still and whisper-barks, "You are not ditching me on prom night. I want you to escort me to the stage when they announce my name."

I let out a disgusted scoff. "Is that all you care about?"

"I didn't have to say yes to you, you know."

I shake her off me with a sharp flick of my arm and pull my jacket straight. "Prom's about hanging out with your friends and celebrating an awesome year. So, why am I over here dancing with you when all I really want to do is hang out with the people I care about?"

She blanches, flashing me a warning look that I'll no doubt regret in the morning.

I don't give a shit.

"I'll see you later, Rox."

And just like that, I turn and walk away from the one thing I've been working for all year.

A large smile engulfs my face.

Man, I've been such a dickhead.

Heading for the exit, I pick up the pace. As much as I want to spend the night with my friends, there's a certain friend who has to be there too.

Careening around the corner, I bump into Tori, nearly knocking her off her feet. I catch her arm, but Colt's right behind her, his hand steadying her against his side.

"Sorry," I mutter, about to move past them.

"Where are you going?" Colt calls after me.

I turn to him with a dopey smile. "I asked the wrong girl to prom."

Tori gasps, then lets out this little squeal. "Oh my gosh." Her hands shake in the air. "I was so hoping you'd see the light. After you guys had that massive fight the other day, I didn't know if you'd be able to overcome it, you know? But then there was just so much chemistry in the air between you and I was thinking, are you blind? Come on, you guys! But now you're leaving prom to go and get her and it's just so romantic. And I—"

"Baby." Colt shuts her up with a soft whisper in her ear.

"Sorry, I'm just excited." She waves her hand toward the doors. "Go! Go, go, go!"

Colt gives her an adoring smile while I shake my head and laugh.

"Good luck, man."

I grin at Colt and bob my head. "Thanks."

Spinning around, I run for the exit, wishing the guys

could be there to celebrate. I highly doubt I'll be able to get Sammy to prom, and I don't even know if I want to. Not with Roxy prowling the room.

That's when an idea hits me. My smile grows to full beam as I yank out my phone. The night's still young and if I can have my way, there's still time to make it the best night ever.

26

GLASSY EYES AND BIG CONFESSIONS

SAMMY

MY TEARS HAVE DRIED up and I'm now left with a pounding headache. See, this is why I don't cry. There's nothing nice about it.

Digging a knuckle into my eye, I rub away the last of my tears and sit up, resting my head against the wood.

Axel's stopped barking and is no doubt keeping watch at the base of the tree. I love how much that dog loves me. I also think it's kind of sad that he's about the only thing that does.

"A dog," I mutter, shaking my head. "Shit, I'm never going to get a boyfriend."

Do I even want one? They seem like more trouble than they're worth.

But then I think of Tyler's kiss and my insides turn to putty again. Pulling my knees to my chest, I perch my cast on top of them and run my finger over the black mesh coating. I can't wait to get this stupid thing off. To get my life back.

But I won't really, will I?

Because things with Tyler and me have been irreparably damaged and tomorrow, after prom, I have to face off with my sister about the photos on her camera. She's probably deleted them already, worried that I was lying when I asked to borrow her camera that day. I need to sneak into her room again. Hell, I should be doing it right now, but I'm feeling too sad, and the idea of going home and bumping into my mother is a little too much to handle.

I don't want anyone to know I've been crying.

Gently pressing the soft tissue beneath my eye, I try to figure out how puffy I'm looking.

Ugh, what an incredibly girly thing to think.

"Do my eyes look puffy?" I mock Roxy's voice, then roll my eyes.

She's right. I'm such a she-man, but it's not like I had much of a choice. Female stuff doesn't come naturally to me. I'm far more comfortable hanging with the guys. That doesn't mean I don't find them attractive, though…and that I don't daydream about making out with Tyler and holding his hand when we walk down the street.

Gliding my fingers over my knuckles, I imagine what it'd feel like to have his strong digits nestled between mine.

"I don't think it'd be so bad," I murmur, then flinch when Axel starts barking.

Scrambling to my knees, I peek out the square window in the treehouse wall and strain to see lights coming on in the house. I don't want anyone knowing I'm up here, but sneaking out with Axel and his giveaway bark is going to be nearly impossible.

I strain to hear noises and am confused when Axel stops barking. I don't want to peek my head right out the window in case someone spots me, so I press my ear against the wood and wait it out. The mechanical sound of the garage door opening makes me cringe.

"Shit, they're home." Lightly thumping my head against the wood, I start to formulate my sneak-out plan. I know the backyard well enough to stick to the shadows. I could even vault the back fence and sneak through the neighbor's yard, then pop out on Pitt Street. It'll take me a little longer to walk home that way, but I'm a big girl and it's not like I'm afraid of the dark.

With a grim frown, I spin around to shuffle to the ladder and yelp when a soft lantern illuminates the space I'm aiming for. Tyler appears, his face cast in ghoulish shadows.

"Holy crap!" I yell, then smack him in the arm when he starts laughing at me. "You just scared the shit out of me. What are you doing here?"

My hammering heart can barely hear his answer. I'm still recovering.

He crawls into the spare space, hanging the torch-lantern on the rusty nail we banged in years ago before cramming his butt into the corner and resting his elbows on his knees. Our feet are touching, so I pull them away and cross my legs.

Great, now my knee's resting against his calf muscle. I swear this treehouse used to be bigger.

Tyler runs his fingers through his hair and shakes his head at me. "Dude, you know how to make a guy work for it, don't you?"

"What?"

"I've spent the last hour hunting the neighborhood for you. Should have figured you'd come here first."

My face bunches with a frown. "What are you doing here? Aren't you supposed to be with my sister right now?"

His lips flatline, the easy relaxed expression I'm used to tucked away behind a grim intensity. "She did it."

"Did what?" My voice is low with dread.

"She outed Kaija."

"Oh… Yeah, I think I already knew that."

Tyler jerks forward. "How?"

"It's a long story."

"How long have you known?"

"I kind of figured it out at the park the other day."

"You should have told me."

"Yeah, well, you were too busy getting your snarky face on." I give him a tight smile.

He points at his chest. "Only because you were being snarky with me!"

"Excuse me? You started it. Making out with my sister like some porn star and agreeing to wear pink! Come on, Tyler." I lurch forward and yank the tie out of his jacket, giving it a little tug. "This is not who you are."

His strong fingers wrap around mine as I hold his tie in the air. "You should have told me," he growls, but it's not an angry, intense one; more like a husky, gruff kind of growl that has warm tendrils curling through my body.

I stare at our touching hands, hating how much I love the feel of it. I can't keep the tremor from my voice when I finally work up the courage to talk again. "I didn't want to ruin prom. Figured I'd tell you after your big night."

Tyler keeps staring at me…waiting for more.

"I'm sorry, okay. I kind of gave you a heads-up."

"You mean the cryptic 'knife between the shoulder blades' thing?" Tyler scoffs.

I shrug, my jaw working to the side. "Okay, so there are things I need to tell you, but I know how much you've been looking forward to this, and I wanted you to be happy. It couldn't all come out at prom, not with Kaija there and Mack's temper… That thing can be like a whole other person."

Tyler snickers. "The Hulk."

I smile and shake my head as an awkward silence settles between us. I can't handle it for long so soon fill the air with the burning question at the forefront of my mind. "Why'd you leave prom?"

Tyler tips his head back, resting it against the wood. "Well, I thought prom was going to be the best night of the year. I was taking the head cheerleader, the coolest girl in school. My friends would be there, admiring what a legend I was, and I'd be king of the school…for just one night." He lifts his index finger to the sky, then purses his lips and lets out a heavy sigh. "Thing is, it didn't feel like I was hoping it would. I knew I'd made a mistake even before Roxy kind of gave away what she'd done."

Running his hand up my arm, he grips my elbow and gently tugs me onto my knees. Rising to his own knees, he settles in front of me and traces his finger down the side of my face. It kind of tickles, but I can't move right now. I can barely breathe.

"I know I talk a big game and try to act cool all the time, but the truth is…I'm happiest when I'm hanging out with you, Sams. I don't need some smokin'-hot cheerleader when I could be hanging out with my best friend…the prettiest girl I know."

I scoff and look away from him. "That's not true, but okay."

He guides my head back to face him and gives me a challenging look. "Which part's not true?"

For some reason, my cheeks are burning. I swallow and try to find my voice. In the end this raspy kind of whisper pops out. "The part about me being pretty."

He grins. "But you are."

"No." I shake my head.

"Yes." He nods. "And I should know, because I've studied a lot of girls."

I tip my head back with a laugh. "Then why the heck are you calling a she-man pretty?"

Running his hands around the back of my neck, he leans his forehead against mine and whispers, "Because it's the truth. You *are* gorgeous. Like one of those sexy elves from *Lord of the Rings*."

My face bunches with a WTF frown and he just laughs.

"It's true. You're hot and beautiful. I just didn't think to notice because, well... Because you're Sammy. My best friend," he whispers, this look of wonder cresting over his face as he draws a line from the corner of my eye to the edge of my mouth. "You're also amazing and kick-ass on the inside, which makes you a million times better than all those shallow hot chicks I've been trying to chase. They're nothing compared to you."

My eyes start to burn as the conviction in his voice hits me right in the heart.

Holy shit. He actually means what he's saying.

I don't know what to do with this, so in true Sammy-style, I go for a joke. That'll keep things safe, right?

"Please, don't get all romantic on me, okay? It doesn't suit you."

Tyler jolts back with a mild look of surprise, his eyes gleaming. "You don't think I can be romantic?"

"Uh, no."

"Okay, fine. I'm gonna say it then."

I frown. "Say what?"

"You want me to say it? I'll say it."

"I don't want you to say it." I shake my head.

Ignoring me completely, he pulls his shoulders back and tugs on his jacket before clearing his throat and announcing loudly, "Samantha Dean Carmichael, there's a chance I might be in love with you."

My eyes bulge for a second, my mouth gaping open before the giggles get the better of me and I burst out laughing.

"What?" he snaps. "It's the truth!"

"There's a chance you *might* be?" I snort. "Wow, take it back a notch, big guy."

Slumping back on his butt, he pulls my arm, forcing me onto his lap. Here we are again, inches from each other's faces and playing that staring game. "Sammy," he whispers, gliding his finger down my face. "You're ruining my big confession, so shut up and let me finish, okay?"

All I can do is nod.

He keeps drawing tickling patterns on my skin while he talks to me. I don't mind it so much; in fact, I think I kind of never want him to stop doing it.

"Thing is, I think I've always loved you, I just didn't realize that's what it was. And then I kissed you and it was like… whoa. But then you wouldn't look at me and it was awkward and I didn't want to screw up our friendship, so I backed off like a total idiot."

His face bunches with an agonized frown.

I shrug. "Yeah, well, you are kind of an idiot, so…"

Tipping his head with a dry glare, he slaps his hand over my mouth. "Are you hearing me right now? I'm being serious. I think I love you and it's terrifying and electrifying and I don't want it to stop!"

I go still, my eyes glassing with tears.

Seriously? More tears! I'm so done with the crying thing!

And I'm not the only one…

Tyler's eyes round and he moves his hand slowly off my mouth. "Oh, shit, please don't cry. I don't think I'm ready for that."

I sniff and shake my head. "Crying sucks. I'm not gonna cry." My voice wobbles out the words.

"You totally are."

"I'm not!" I try to sit up, but his strong arms pull me down and I'm back to staring into his eyes again. "I just never thought you'd say that to me."

He grins. "Me neither, but I really like that I have."

My lips rise into a smile. I can't help it. Tyler Schumann's giving me the big feels!

"I want to take you to prom."

Ugh.

Big feelings gone.

I screw up my face and start shaking my head. If he honestly thinks I'm going to waltz into prom and have to contend with my sister, he's got another thing coming.

I struggle to get off his knee, but he just laughs and holds me steady.

"Don't make me hit you," I warn. "Seriously, Ty, let me go."

"Not until you say yes."

"I am not going to the prom, you crazy man. Now lemme go."

"Come on, Sammy, you don't even have to get changed."

"Oh, really?" I throw him a skeptical frown, still struggling. "You expect me to show up to prom in ripped jeans and a tear-stained T-shirt? Nice move, Casanova. Not happening."

"It's so happening." He gives me a cocky wink, then bumps me off his knee. I flop to the floor while he shuffles to the window and peeks outside.

I frown and jump to my knees, thumping up behind him and squeezing my head through the gap. My chin drops onto his shoulder as I gaze down into his backyard and spot our friends below. Finn, Tori, and Colt are lighting the outside torches while Kaija is setting up the stereo. Layla appears out the backdoor carrying a tray stacked with Burger King bags, and following in her wake is Mack, holding a massive tub of ice and Coca Cola bottles. Glass ones, my favorite kind.

Axel's muffled bark is coming from the garage. He'll be suffering from major FOMO (fear of missing out) right now. I cringe for him but then Tyler turns to look at me.

"I knew you wouldn't want to come to prom, so I thought I'd bring prom to you." His voice is so sweet right now I want to melt right into it.

Biting my bottom lip, I grab the collar of his suit and spin him around to face me. He flops onto his butt and

I straddle his lap, holding his face in my hands and smiling at him.

"Okay, so maybe I've been in love with you since second grade."

"Seriously?" His face lights up with a triumphant grin. "Wow. That's pretty cool." He nods. "Kind of hard not to though, right? I mean, what's not to love?"

"Don't push it." I give him a droll glare, which he just starts laughing at.

I love that sound, that low chuckle of his; it rumbles right through me. With a soft snicker, I lean towards him and the sound cuts off.

His soft breath whistles over my skin while my heart accelerates to a pounding rhythm that works through my entire body. I know we've kissed before, but it still feels like a first for me. Tyler's hand softly glides up my back. I press my nose against his and then close that final space between us.

His lips are perfect—soft, pliable, warm…familiar.

My mouth tells me I'm home.

I close my eyes and the outside shuffling below is drowned out as I focus on the music our kisses make. I love the sound of our lips pulling apart, then smacking back together, that soft puff of air as we open our mouths. Tyler's fingers grip the back of my neck as his tongue slides along mine, twisting inside my mouth before ducking away so he can gently suck my bottom lip.

I start to smile as his fingers inch up and weave into my hair, tangling within the long strands and holding me against him. Tipping my head, I deepen the kiss and I swear I could stay on his lap kissing him all night long.

But...

27

A NOT-SO-PERFECT END TO A TOTALLY PERFECT NIGHT

TYLER

"ARE you guys coming down or what?"

I could kill Mack right now.

"Come on, you guys. Let's get this party started!"

And then I'm going to kill Colt.

Sammy's breathy snicker pops into my mouth. I smile against her lips and swipe my tongue along hers one more time.

The music starts blasting from below and I add Kaija to my kill list.

Sammy tries to shift away from me but I resist the move, pulling her back against my lips with a little whine. She laughs and mumbles against my mouth, "Hey, you invited them."

"Worst idea ever," I grumble, kissing her again.

Her fingers curl into my lapels and she lets out this sweet kind of moan. Oh yeah, I could easily get addicted to that sound. I suck her lip and ignore the chant my friends have started up.

"Come on down! Come on down!" They're clapping and everything.

Sammy laughs and pulls far enough away that I can no longer reach her mouth. Pressing her forehead against mine, she whispers, "Hey, if what you said in here is true then there are going to be plenty more chances to kiss me in the future."

I snap my eyes to hers, resting my thumbs on the sides of her face so she can't turn away from me. "I meant it."

"Then we better get our butts down there. You can kiss me tomorrow."

"You can count on it."

"Good." She winks and gives me the brightest smile I've ever seen.

Damn. She really is beautiful.

She heads down first. The second her legs appear on

the ladder, my friends start cheering. Her feet hit the grass and Tori jumps on her, wrapping her twig arms around Sammy's shoulders.

"So glad you could make it." Pixie Girl laughs.

Sammy hugs her back while I bump Colt's fist and mouth, "Thank you."

"Best idea you've ever had, Schumann." Mack smacks my arm with the back of his hand.

Kaija appears beside him. She's taken her tower heels off and her bare toes are peeking out beneath the folds of fabric. Leaning her head on Mack's shoulder, she smiles at me. "You're a legend, mate."

I grin at her kiwi compliment, then turn when Finn slaps me on the back, handing me a burger. "Thanks, man."

"Ooo, double cheese!" Sammy takes the burger from Layla and immediately unwraps it. "I'm starving." Taking a monster bite, she turns to me with a grin. The food bunches in her cheeks, making her look like a chipmunk. Her eyes sparkle as she steps over to me and takes a seat at my feet, crossing her legs and chowing down.

Finn spreads out a few blankets and my backyard is soon a picnic area filled with elegant prom dresses, glittering jewelry, and a whole lot of laughs.

I stay close to Sammy the whole night, touching her whenever I can—resting my knee on hers as we eat side-by-side, touching her lower back as we walk over to grab two bottles of Coke, wrapping my arms around her as the couples break off and start slow dancing in the grass.

She looks radiant beneath the stars, smiling up at me with that dreamy look on her face. I waste no time and kiss her while I can. The music washes over us as each couple gets lost in their little loved-up moments. It's the world's most perfect prom. We don't need some fake night under the stars when we can have it for real.

I look up at the night sky, my mind moving ahead to the summer break. It's going to be freaking awesome. I'm totally inviting Sammy to Myrtle Beach with us.

The phone in her back pocket buzzes; I can feel the vibration with my pinky finger. She ignores it and keeps swaying...until it buzzes again. Yanking it out with a huff, she perches the phone on my shoulder, still swaying as she clears the message.

But then she stops.

I glance at her face, instant worry coursing through me.

"You alright?"

"Yeah," she whispers in my ear. "I've just got to get home. Shit's hitting the fan already."

I pull back to get a better look at her face. Her eyes are stormy with angst, and I have a sinking feeling that whatever she's hiding isn't going to be pretty.

"Um…" She clears her throat and looks over her shoulder. "Sorry, guys, I've got to go." She waves her phone in the air. "Mom's looking for me."

Finn checks his watch and winces. "It's past two. I gotta get you home, pretty lady." He glides his finger down Layla's cheek and kisses the end of her nose. She gives him a disappointed smile, but he wipes it away with his lips.

"I'll walk you home." I raise my chin at the gate, then look to Mack. "Just leave everything. I'll deal with it in the morning."

"Okay, man. Thanks for a good night."

I smile at my friends, trying to hide my worry for Sam. I don't know what shit she's talking about. I just have a sick feeling in my gut that's telling me it's bad.

She's already walking around the side of the house and I run to catch up with her. As soon as she's pushed the phone back into her pocket, I capture her hand and thread my fingers between hers. She looks down at our interlinking digits with a soft smile.

"So, what did the text say?"

Her smile turns to a frown. "Just from my mom,

wanting to know where I am and why you ditched Roxy at prom. *'If you're with that Tyler boy, there's going to be trouble. I don't want you hanging out with someone who ditches his date.'*" She puts on a voice and rolls her eyes.

I watch her face carefully, waiting for more. I can tell by the tightening at the edge of her mouth that she's holding out on me.

"Something else is going on. What aren't you saying?"

"You don't want to know. Trust me." Sammy raises her eyebrows. "Let's just say Roxy won't let this prom thing slide. She's probably in her room plotting first-degree murder right now."

I huff out a cynical laugh and shake my head. "I knew I'd pay for this choice." I squeeze her hand, needing her to know I was happy to do it. "Don't worry about it. I can handle Roxy."

She huffs and looks up at the stars with a groan. "You don't know what you're saying. You don't...know," she ends with a breathy whisper.

I jerk her to a stop and frown down at her. "Sammy, enough. Tell me the truth, right now."

Her eyes dart to mine and then up to the sky again before she dips her head and tries to hide behind her hair. I bend low, sweeping her long locks over her shoulder and forcing her to look me in the eye.

Her blue eyes, usually so sharp and strong, are glassy with tears. "She took the photos, Tyler."

"What?"

"Roxy is the party paparazzo. I found the shots on her camera. At first, I thought maybe someone borrowed it, because I never see Roxy using the thing, but after Dana told me Roxy took photos of Kaija's diary, I knew…" She shakes her head.

"Wait a second… What?" My voice is sharp with confusion. "Are you saying that not only is Roxy the one who outed Kaija, but she also took those photos of her *best friend* being mauled by those guys?"

"They're pretty bad, right?" Sammy whispers.

"Yeah," I huff, anger grating down my spine as the images flash through my brain. "You saw them all?"

She catches my eye. The grave frown on her face makes my gut pinch tight. "Actually, I'm wondering if I've seen more than you."

"What does that mean?"

Sammy bites the corner of her lip and looks to the ground. I squeeze her hand, silently asking her to spill.

"When you first told me about the photos, I kind of got the impression that Layla was drunk and mistakenly got into it… You know, like she wanted to get it on with Derek and Quaid."

She pauses and I prompt her with a quiet, "But…"

"I'll admit that I was looking through the back of a camera screen, so it was small, but the last shot I saw before having to put the camera away…" She shakes her head. "Layla wasn't happy."

I feel like I've just been punched in the gut. A puff of air spurts out of my mouth and I grip Sammy's hand so tight she lets out a little squeak.

"Sorry." I let her go, stepping back so far I nearly stumble onto the road.

Catching myself, I pace back into Sammy's space and give her an agonized frown.

"Are you saying that…like, did they roofie her or something?"

"I don't know. I just…" She huffs. "In the photo, her face is kind of bunched like she wants out and they're not letting her."

I run a hand through my hair, scratching the back of my head as I recapture the images I printed for Finn when it all went down. "You couldn't see her face. Maybe the side, but never a shot of her whole face." I grip my mouth and mumble into it. "Shit, Sammy, this is bad."

"I know." Her lips bunch into a tight line. "And I'm so ashamed that my sister's involved. I don't know why she did it. The Kaija thing was pure jealousy, but why Layla?"

I shrug, completely short of answers. Roxy's turning out to be one crazy-ass bitch. I can't even begin to figure out what's going on in that psycho brain of hers.

"Layla needs to know that truth," Sammy whispers.

I stare at her puckered frown and then reach for her hand, giving it a gentle squeeze. "Yeah, I know. And don't kill me for saying this, but then we need to take your sister down."

Sammy clenches her jaw and nods.

It's not exactly the perfect end to a perfect night. I finally figure out how I feel about this girl and of course it has to be her sister who turns out to be completely insane. She potentially poses a big threat, but I refuse to be put off by that.

I close the gap between us until our bodies are melded together. Locking my fingers behind Sammy's back, I gaze down at her and make her a silent promise.

No fight's too big. I know what I want now, and I'll defend us with everything I've got.

28

UGLY TEARS IN THE BURGERHOUSE

SAMMY

"WELL, well, well, look who's home." Roxy's voice is sticky sweet and fake as plastic.

I stiffen but keep trudging up the stairs.

"Have a good night, sister?" She leans over the banister and I glance up, spotting the crown perched on her head.

Biting my lips against her snarky tone, I keep going and brush right past her when she tries to block my way at the top of the stairs.

"I know you guys were together. I've made sure Mom does too. She's not impressed that you're hanging out with a jerk who dumps his date on the biggest night of her year. Thanks to you all ditching us, Darius was crowned king and I had to dance with his sorry ass while he grinned at me with this dopey smile."

"Don't know why you're complaining. Darius is a good dancer," I mutter.

She snatches my arm, digging her nails in as she spins me around to face her. "It was humiliating," she seethes. "Standing on that stage as Mack, then Colt, then Tyler's names were called out. All people could talk about was why they left prom."

"Aw, poor Roxy. Was the attention off you for a second? That must have really sucked." I pry her hand off my arm and gently shove her away from me.

"How dare you." Her whisper is dark with malice. "You should all know better than to ditch me on the most important night of my life."

Stopping at my door, I press my fingers into the wood and try to slow my racing heart

"You're all going to pay for it. I don't care who I have to trample to make my point."

I spin around, narrowing my eyes at her. "Are you admitting something to me, Roxanne?"

She blinks, her face transforming into a look of pure innocence. "I'm not sure what you're talking about."

I let out a disgusted huff and scowl at her.

Her eyes gleam with a wicked grin. "I guess it's safe to admit now that the only reason I said yes to that loud-mouthed idiot was to irritate you."

My eyes narrow into a warning glare.

"Worked for a while." She grins. "But I guess your she-man scent overpowered him or something." Licking the edge of her mouth, she winks at me. "Hope you enjoyed that tongue of his; it's the only good thing about him."

It takes every ounce of willpower I possess, but I manage to paste on a smile and reply in a calm voice, "Too bad for you that's total bullshit. He's more than you will ever know...more than you'll ever deserve."

"Don't get cocky, little sister. Just enjoy the win tonight, because it's the last one you're going to get."

"Watch out, Roxanne. Your nasty side is showing through. Wouldn't want to shatter the illusion now, would we?"

She smirks. "I'm not worried for me." Her eyes glitter. "But tell your boyfriend to watch his back. I'm going to start with him."

My eyes flash wide and I point my finger at her. "You touch him and I will—"

"Night, night," she sings, wiggling her fingers at me and skipping off to her room.

A deep growl reverberates in my throat and I'm tempted to smash her door down and finish my threat for real.

But what's the point?

I'm not into beating up girls, even ones as evil as my sister.

Ugh! I can't believe we're related!

No, the best way to beat her is to expose her for what she really is.

It's gonna hurt, but it has to happen. Roxy needs to be stopped before she does any more damage. It's time to quit skirting the issue and deal with it head-on.

I spin for my room but am stopped by the last voice I want to hear.

"Samantha? Is that you?" Mom calls from her bedroom.

"Uh, yeah?"

"Come in here. We need to talk."

With a deep cringe, I head for Mom's doorway, preparing myself for the inevitable lecture. Kind of sucks that the perfect night has to end this way. I doubt I'm going to get much sleep. If Mom's standard dress-down isn't enough to keep me wide awake, the thought of telling Layla the truth will definitely do it.

Briggs' Burgerhouse is often busy on a Sunday morning. They introduced a brunch menu last summer and it was a real hit. The place just keeps getting busier, which is so not helping me today.

I glance at Tyler with a worried frown. "Do you think we should do this somewhere else?"

He shakes his head, leading me to the booth where Layla's sitting. "We've got to get it out of the way. We have to move fast before Roxy hurts anyone else."

I'm so glad I told him everything. I didn't even wait until the morning, calling him as soon as I got back to my room. We talked until four o'clock in the morning, and then I lay in bed worrying about today. Tyler's right, we have to act fast. I don't know what my sister has planned for him, but we need to arm ourselves against whatever attack she's going to throw at us.

Man, I wish I didn't have to do this.

Roxy's a bad person, there's no denying this, but she's still my sister and it feels weird plotting against her. I don't mind a little competition, but a full-on takedown?

Layla's in the booth, scanning the menu. Her long dark hair is glossy and smooth, unlike mine. I run my fingers through the limp strands and give my hair a sniff. Thankfully, it still smells okay. I ended up falling asleep

267

at like seven this morning and when I was jolted awake by Ty's phone call, I only had five minutes to get ready.

I rub my cast and scan the empty booth.

"Where's everyone else?" I blurt way louder than I mean to.

Layla glances up and gives me a tired smile. "They're coming. Kaija forgot something back at the house, so they dropped me and went home to get it."

I slide into the booth and shuffle around until I'm sitting next to the dark-haired beauty. She smells like flowers; whatever perfume she's wearing is sweet and tickles my nose. I rub my finger under my nostrils and clench my jaw.

How am I going to tell her? How do I even form the words?

Maybe it's a good thing that we've got her on her own. She can get over the initial shock without everyone else gaping at her.

Tyler nudges my shoulder and lifts his chin at Layla who is reading the menu. I make a reluctant face, but he just bulges his eyes at me and mouths, "Do it."

Clearing my throat, I rest my arms on the table and force a smile when Layla's brown eyes pop up to meet mine.

"So...um..." My chest deflates.

Layla gives me a quizzical frown. "What's going on?"

I don't miss the flash of fear in her eyes. Does she know what I'm about to say? Can she see it on my face?

Slapping the menu onto the table, she gives me this intense kind of stare, forcing the words out of me.

"You know the photos of you and...?"

She jerks back, her body pinging tight, a tendon in her neck flexing as she throws a warning look at Tyler. "How do you know about that?"

"I told her." His voice is deep and husky.

Her wide-eyed warning morphs into a fierce scowl.

"I'm sorry," he murmurs. "But I was trying to find the party paparazzo and I knew Sammy could help me."

"I thought we were letting this go." Her voice pitches.

"I know." Tyler taps the table. "But I couldn't just turn my back. I was worried that..."

Layla's shocked, sick expression kills Tyler's explanation, so I jump in before she can flee the booth.

"I found more photos."

Her skin goes white, her brown eyes swirling with

agony as she snaps, "What? Where? Were they posted online? Has anyone else seen them?" Her voice is getting high and borderline hysterical.

I put my hand on her arm, trying to calm her down. "No, nothing like that. I found them on a camera. As far as I know, no one else has seen them."

She sags back into the seat but her breathing is still erratic.

"I'm sorry, Layla. I know you don't want to hear this, but you have to know the truth," I speak quickly.

"What truth?" Her voice is small and quaking as she looks at me with big, scared eyes that make me think of a young child about to get screamed at by her parents.

I swallow and then whisper, "You weren't into it."

Her forehead wrinkles. "What?"

"You weren't into it," I repeat, loud and clear so I know she's definitely heard me.

She goes still for a second, like a porcelain statue, and then very slowly she covers her mouth with quivering fingers. Her eyes fill with tears when she turns to look at me. "What are you saying?"

"I saw your face. You weren't..." I shake my head. "You did *not* want Quaid and Derek touching you like that."

Layla puffs out a sharp breath and sucks it in again, her

270

chest heaving like she's about to hyperventilate, but then the breaths morph to sobs. Her face bunches as tears spill from her eyes and she starts crying. And I don't just mean those silent petite tears, but full-blown ugly crying.

My mouth opens and closes as I fight for the right words to calm her. The people at the table closest to us turn to investigate the noise. I throw them a weak smile, then start patting Layla's shoulder and murmuring, "It's okay. Um…"

I look to Tyler for support, but all he can do is give me an awkward kind of shrug.

I thought the news would be a relief to her and totally don't understand what's going on right now…or how to fix it.

29

THIS CAN'T STAND

TYLER

I CAN'T JUST SIT HERE LISTENING to Layla cry. Shuffling out of the booth, I move around the table and am about to slide in and offer what comfort I can when Finn's deep voice stops me.

"What the...?" He yanks my shirt and pulls me away from the table. "What did you do?"

"Nothing. I..."

He slides into the booth, pulling Layla against his side as soon as she's within reach. "I'm here, baby. What's wrong?" he whispers in her ear.

She wraps her arms around him and presses her forehead into his neck. He rubs her back up and down, murmuring something I can't hear. Thankfully, it doesn't take him too long to coax her out of her cry-fest.

I shuffle along the round booth until my knee is pressed against Sam's. Not a big one for crying, she's looking way awkward right now. Thank God Finn showed up.

He throws me a dark look over Layla's head while he waits for her to tell him what's up.

"I wasn't into it," she murmurs, just as Tori and Colt arrive.

"Hey." Tori's bright smile is cut in half as soon as she spots Layla. She gasps. "Oh, no. What happened?"

She slides in next to me and reaches across the table. Layla grasps her fingers and I look at their linked arms, struck by how much things have changed. It's kind of comforting, to be honest.

"I wasn't into it," Layla repeats, her voice growing in confidence.

Colt gives her a bemused frown.

"At the party," she murmurs.

"Are you talking about...?" He glances at Sammy, then me.

"She knows," I tell him.

"Knows what?" Mack slides into the booth and smiles at me before catching Layla's face and instantly frowning. "What's going on?"

Kaija slides in next to him, resting her hand on his shoulder while carefully eyeing each person at the table.

I let out a sigh, about to spill the beans, but Sammy steps up before I can.

"Okay, here it is. Tyler wasn't happy about the fact you guys didn't want to find out who the party paparazzo was. He was worried that if you did nothing the photos would come out at some point, so I agreed to help him track the…person down."

"And? Anything?" Mack's intense gaze is boring into Sammy.

I try to throw him a warning look but he doesn't notice me so I just blurt, "Tone it down, man." His gaze darts to me and I face it head-on. "Sammy found some more photos."

"And I wasn't into it," Layla interjects, leaning her head back to rest against Finn's arm. "I wasn't into it. Thank God," she whispers, covering her face with her hands.

That's when the lightbulb suddenly flicks on for everyone. Tori gasps while Finn's lips part in horror, then quickly bunch with rage.

"Where'd you find these photos?" Colt's question is deep and intense, matching the entire tone of the table.

I look to Sammy, who nervously licks her lips. Her eyes dart to Layla, then back to the tabletop. "On Roxy's camera. Along with pictures of Kaija's diary."

The news cuts off the air supply in the room. I swear, man, it's like impossible to breathe right now.

Kiwi Girl's the first to inhale. Her forehead wrinkles with confusion and then she spits out the words with more venom than I've ever seen. "That bitch!"

Sammy nods, her cheeks flaring red.

"Roxy?" Layla's eyes are the size of dinner plates. "You mean, like my best friend Roxy?"

"She is not getting away with this." Kaija slaps the table. "How the hell did she even get my diary?"

Sammy gives her a pained kind of smile. "Dana found it under your mattress and then she got onto Facebook with—"

"Anna." Kaija finishes for me. "Those little toe rags! And now she's gone after Layla too?"

"I don't know why." Sammy shrugs. "I wanted to think the best of her, like maybe someone had used her camera without knowing, but..." She lets out a heavy sigh, her shoulders drooping.

"Frickin' Dana," Mack grumbles. "What the hell was she thinking?"

"Hey, I know it was crazy stupid, but she's really scared now." Sammy taps the table to get Mack's attention. "Roxy's threatened to do some pretty nasty stuff if she blabs about it. She knows she's in the wrong, and she feels really bad."

"Well, that's just great, but it still doesn't change the fact that Kaija was completely humiliated and she's partly to blame!"

"And she's scared shitless, so back off, man."

"Why are you standing up for her?" Mack thumps the table.

"Hey!" I snap my fingers between them. "Stay on point. We've got photos to deal with too."

Mack's nostrils flare as he slumps back against the padded booth. Kaija rubs his shoulder with a tight smile, obviously just as riled as Mack.

"Do you think she set Layla up, or was it just an opportune moment?" Finn's voice is so low it's almost hard to hear him. He's curling the edge of the menu with his finger, staring at the tabletop and obviously working to stay calm.

"It had to be a setup," Layla whispers. "Why else would she have taken her camera to that party?"

Colt makes a face. "Does that mean she knows Derek?"

"How?" Layla shakes her head. "When would she ever see him?"

"I don't know." Colt shrugs. "At parties and stuff. She goes to enough of them."

"This is so messed up," Tori whispers. "Layla. Kaija. I'm so sorry about all of this. It sucks."

The girls both look at Tori, unable to help smiling at the sweet girl. I lightly nudge her with my elbow and grin, letting her know how much I've come to like her.

"We can't let this stand." Mack's voice cuts through the fleeting moment of sweetness.

"I know." Sammy nods. "She's pissed at you guys for ditching her last night and she's going after Tyler first. I don't know what she plans on doing, but our best chance is to get that proof before she can do anything nasty with it. We need dirt on her. That's the only thing that will keep us safe."

"Do you think it'll still be on her camera?" Kaija asks.

"I'm not sure." Sammy shrugs, the edge of her mouth tipping up in a fleeting grin. "But there's only one way to find out."

30

DISGUSTING REVELATIONS

SAMMY

I WALK UP my driveway and hide my board by the shed. It was a big risk taking it today after my painful lecture from Mom last night, but it was an easy ride to Briggs' and back. I figured that could be my argument if she busted me. Tyler had already tried to tell me off, but I just rolled my eyes at him.

After the total downer of a meal, where most of the time was spent not eating and talking about how horrible my sister is, we parted ways. Everyone's exhausted, and all I really want to do is catch a few Zs before figuring out how I'm going to get those photos from Roxy. Hopefully they're still on her camera. That'd be easy. I could just grab it out of her drawer and take off. I'd have all the proof I need to...

To what?

Stop her? Challenge her? Make her apologize?

I snort.

Yeah, like that would ever happen. I'm pretty sure the word 'sorry' isn't even in her vocabulary. At least not the genuine kind of apology Layla and Kaija both deserve.

With a heavy sigh, I thump up the stairs. The house is really quiet, which means Mom's out and Roxy's probably still sleeping off last night.

Hell, I should sneak in and grab the pics now, but I'm not bold enough to commando crawl past her bed while she snoozes. What if I wake her up?

I'm still trying to figure out what we'll do once we get the photos. Layla wants them destroyed…that's it. But Mack countered that we need to find out all the other places they might be. Wiping them off Roxy's camera isn't enough; we need to go to the source and kill it that way.

He was pretty vehement when he was speaking and most people around the table were bobbing their heads, in agreement.

I'm cool with getting rid of the photos and yes, Roxy needs to pay, but…she's still my sister.

I don't even get why I'm wrestling with this. My sister is a first-class bitch. I wish I could one hundred percent hate her. It should be easy enough to do. It just feels so wrong to make an enemy of my own flesh and blood.

Stopping at the top of the stairs, I gaze at her door with a sad frown before heading for my bedroom.

The shower's running.

I stop.

Wait a second.

Staring at the bathroom door, my ears burn as I listen for sounds around the house. If Mom's out, which I'm positive she is, then Roxy must be the one in the shower...which means I should totally sneak in and grab her camera now.

It's not the plan. Layla's going to distract her after school tomorrow so Tyler and I can come home, hunt through Roxy's room, and get what we need, but...

She's in the shower!

I have a clear shot, right now. I should totally take it.

Biting my lip, I ignore all caution and head for my sister's room.

Caution's for pussies anyway, right?

With a little smirk, I ease her door open and tiptoe

inside. Rushing to her desk, I drop to my knees and pull her camera out of its hiding place. Thank God. It's exactly where I left it, which means she doesn't suspect that I know anything.

Holding my breath, I turn it on and push the button to scroll through the photos, my face wrinkling when I spot the *no memory card* warning. Shit! I turn the camera over and look for the place the memory card is stored, hoping it's just a camera malfunction. I flick it open and spot the battery, but no memory card.

Dammit!

Where the hell would she have put it?

Scrambling back to my feet, I start rifling through her desk, digging in to drawers and disrupting their contents. I don't even care that I'm making a mess; I just want to find that card and get out of here.

I find nothing in the desk.

Double dammit.

Spinning around, I scan her room, looking for memory card hiding places. It's probably not even in here. She's probably buried it somewhere I'll never be able to find it. Huffing out a sharp breath, I stomp to her bed and grab pillows, slapping the mattress, bending low to dig beneath it

Nothing.

Scanning the walls, I consider tearing off posters, wondering if it'll be stuck behind one of them, but then my eyes catch her jewelry box.

"Oh, please be in there."

Scrambling over her bed, not caring that my shoes are no doubt leaving marks on her rumpled white sheets, I jerk to a stop against her dresser drawers and open up the intricate wooden box. It opens like a miniature closet and I pull at the tiny drawers, sweeping my finger through the contents. Rings and fine necklaces clink together, the metal sounds disappointing me until I reach the bottom drawer and I hear the clunk of hard plastic.

I suck in a breath and pull the drawer all the way out, a relieved smile cresting my lips as I stare down at the memory card.

"We've got you now," I whisper, my mind jumping to the photos on the card. Disgust surges through me as I recapture the distress on Layla's face and Quaid and Derek's greedy hands on her body. "You asshats are going down."

Wrestling the memory card out of the small drawer, I'm about to slide everything back into place when I hear the bathroom door click open.

Shit!

Gripping the card, I try to shove the drawer back into place, but my angle's wrong and it jams. Holding my breath, I pull it out and carefully slide it back into place before slamming the box shut. My plan is to dive under the bed and hide, but I run out of time before the door creaks open.

"What are you doing home?" The voice is male, foreign to my ears, and has this harsh bite to it.

Totally confused, I spin to face the last person I ever expected to see in my house. My mouth drops open, my eyes bugging out big time as I take in Derek—wearing nothing but a pair of jeans and a towel draped around his neck. His hair is still shiny with moisture.

I frown at him, still trying to figure out why this asshole is even in my house, let alone *wet* in my house.

"What are you doing here?"

His cheeks flare with color, and it's only then that I notice the shower's still running.

Ew. It's still running...and he's wet...with a towel, which means he probably just got out and...

Gross!

I swallow and stick out my tongue like I'm about to gag.

"Okay, so that's disgusting. You and my sister?"

He shrugs. "We kind of can't resist each other. Why fight something you know is right?"

I shudder. "Foul factor like one billion."

"Don't judge until you've tasted." He licks his lips. "Your sister knows a good thing when she sees it."

"Her tongue was down another guy's throat less than twenty-four hours ago."

"Yeah, but that was only to piss you off. I don't mind sharing if it's for a good cause." Pulling the towel off his shoulder, he slaps it onto the end of the bed, giving me full view of his cut torso.

Okay, so he's got a nice body, but the charred soul inside it makes it basically impossible to find him attractive.

What a douche.

The shower turns off with a clunk. It's always done that. The pipes in the house let out this soft kind of whine and I know my sister's about done.

She's going to waltz in here any second, and I can't be caught with this memory card in my hand. The hair dryer starts up, buying me another few minutes, but I still need to get out of here.

"Well." I clear my throat. "As obscene as this revelation has been, I'm gonna get going. I've got some puking to do, and my eyes are in serious need of sterilization."

I grimace at his bare torso then slip the card into my back pocket and try to casually walk for the door. I've just passed Derek and think I'm home free when his hand clamps around my wrist and he jerks me to a stop.

"What've you got in your pocket?" Dragging me against him, he starts feeling up my ass, looking for the card. His nostrils are flaring, warning me he knows exactly what I've got in my pocket.

I shove at his chest with my cast, but he's stronger than I anticipated and I end up having to stomp on his bare foot. His arms slacken as he growls and I take the chance to slip out of his grasp.

"Get back here!" he roars.

The thunderous sound jolts me and I vault over the railing, hurting my wrist and landing with a thud on the middle of the stairwell. He crashes against the banister and glares down at me.

I glower right back, refusing to show my fear, then jump down the rest of the stairs. Flinging the door open, I take off onto the street, heading straight to Tyler's place.

31

AN ALLEY BRAWL

TYLER

FINN TOSSES me the ball and I catch it against my chest, wandering up the grass on Steinway Field before throwing the ball to Colt. He catches it with a frown and lobs it across to Finn. We're not talking as we try to blow off steam at the park. As soon as Colt dropped me home, I grabbed my bike and cycled the streets. I headed to the ramp and messed around while I waited for Sammy to wake from her nap and call me. It ended up being Colt who called first. He was restless, and I told him to meet me here so we could blow off some steam. He turned up with Finn and we started chucking the ball around.

To be honest, it's not really working. We're just robotically hurling the ball through the air, caught up in our own unrest.

This morning's breakfast was depressing, sobering…so not the way I pictured this weekend going.

Sammy's truth bomb is pretty heinous. Layla looked like she was in shock, trying to process how her best friend could betray her. She couldn't even reach anger. I hope she's managing a rest after all that crying.

Mack and Kaija have gone to have some time alone before she heads back to New Zealand in a few days. I'm so glad my girl's sticking around.

I catch the ball with a small grin.

My girl.

I kind of like thinking of Sammy that way. I mean, she always has been, but now it's on a whole new level. I can't wait to see what we get up to over the summer. She's already said yes to my Myrtle Beach invitation. I asked her when we were kissing goodbye at the restaurant, hoping to cheer her up some. It kind of worked. It's something to look forward to anyway. We can hang out, be a couple, have some laughs.

My girlfriend is my best friend.

It's freaking awesome.

I lift my arm and send a sweet spiral to Colt, imagining

Sammy curled up on her bed, trying to catch some shut-eye. She looked pretty tired this morning. Hell, I'm still tired, but sleeping's the last thing I can do. I'm too wired. Maybe if I went and snuggled up with Sam I could find the head space to switch off and sleep.

Tempting.

But I doubt her mom would be too impressed, and I'm not really in the frame of mind to see Roxy.

I let out a derisive snort and watch Finn run to catch the ball. He cradles it against his chest and is about to throw it my way when my phone starts ringing. I raise my hand for him to stop and dig the phone out of my back pocket.

Sammy's name is on my screen and I answer with a grin.

"'Sup, Skater Girl?"

"So I think it's safe to say they know each other!" she yells into the phone. She sounds like she's out of breath.

My face bunches with confusion. "Who are you talking about?"

"Derek and Roxy! I just found him shirtless in her bedroom!"

"Shit, no way." I glance up at Colt and Finn, who have

now walked over to find out what's going on. "Derek and Roxy have been hooking up," I tell them.

Colt's eyes bulge while Finn's dark eyebrows knit together. I press the phone to my ear, about to ask for more info, when I notice that Sammy's breathing is only getting heavier.

"Are you running right now?"

"He's chasing me..." She puffs. "And he looks pretty pissed."

My insides jolt like I've just been slapped in the face.

"Where are you?" I snap.

"Heading to your place," she puffs. "I'm coming out the alley off Fletcher Street. I've got the photos and... Shit!"

There's an oomph, a clatter, and then the line goes dead.

My heart jerks to a stop and I gape at the phone for a split second before hauling ass to my bike.

"Where are you going?" Finn calls out to me.

"Sammy's in trouble!" I grab my bike and jump on. "Take the truck to Millhouse Road! She's in the alley off Fletcher!"

I start pedaling before they can ask for more details. All

I can focus on is getting to Sammy. Hearing her yell into the phone like that frickin' sucked. What's Derek doing to her right now?

I'm going to kill him for ever touching her.

He shouldn't even be in Nelson. The guy's on freaking probation. Ballsy asshole. I can't wait to crunch my knuckles into his face.

Pumping the pedals, I fly off the curb and swerve in the middle of the street. I think I break every bike law in the state trying to reach Sammy, but I don't give a shit.

The wheels scrape along the concrete as I take a tight left into the maze of alleys that connects the various cul-de-sacs in my area. I know exactly which alley Sammy's in, and I hear the scuffling before I even get sight of them.

Not even bothering to brake, I jump off the bike and let it skid into the fence, then run full tilt at Derek who is yanking on Sammy's ankle as she tries to get to her feet and run. There's blood on her lips, but she's looking damn fierce as she throws her broken arm back, smashing his cheek with her cast.

"Ow!" she cries out, clutching her arm to her chest and flopping to the ground.

I ready my fist and plow it into Derek's other cheek as

he staggers to his feet. He flies back the other way, crashing into the fence.

Bracing himself against the wood, he shakes his dazed head and lurches back to try for a fight. Blood is oozing from both his nostrils and there's a red welt forming below his right eye.

"Give me that card," he slurs. "And I might let you live."

Sammy groans. "You are such a douche!" Her voice stretches tight over the words, giving away how much her punch hurt her. "Aren't you tired of girls making you bleed? Give up and take your sorry ass home!"

He snarls and lunges at her. I jump forward and push him back against the fence. I wish he was wearing a shirt so I could fist his collar and get in his face. I have to suffice with shoving his sweaty chest when he tries to lurch forward again.

"Home's too good for an asshole like you," I seethe.

He makes a move to split but I block his way, shoving him back again. I don't want this slippery turd getting away from us, but I'm also hyperaware that Sammy is lying on the ground behind me...in pain. I've got to get her to the hospital.

Derek glares at me, his black rage so potent it's almost making my eyes water. He may be beat down right now, but he's going to lunge again and I need to protect Sammy. I shift so I'm right in front of her, aware of the fist Derek is forming.

Picturing what could happen, I decide that being in front of Sam is probably not the best move. I need to draw the guy away so she'll be out of range. Shuffling slowly, I maneuver into a safer zone, hoping he'll go after me and not strike at her again.

He's still trying to take me down with his venomous grimace, but I'm not backing away from this fight.

I will him to get on with it already and he reads my mind, letting out a low growl and coming at me like a rabid dog. Raising my arm, I block his attack, then strike out with my fist. It clips him in the chin, but barely enough to move him. He counters with a power punch that captures me in the side, then follows through with a solid left cross. Damn, the guy's faster than I thought he'd be. His knuckles catch me in the cheek, knocking me sideways. My hands slap against the fence and I use the momentum to push myself back up, swiveling around with a powerful left hook.

I finally strike him properly and he stumbles back, but the move only enrages him. He snarls, acting like the frickin' Hulk as he lunges forward, tackling me to the ground and pounding my side with his fist. I wrestle to free myself, grunting as he catches a good hit to my back.

"Get off him!" Sammy shouts, jumping on Derek's back and yanking his hair. He raises his shoulder, trying to flick her off, but she's a spider monkey, her legs wrapping around his hips. He struggles to stand, running backwards and smashing her into the fence.

"No!" I shout as her eyes glass with pain.

He steps forward so she can slump to the ground, then spins and grabs her cast. She screams as he tries to bash it into the fence but I'm on him, wrapping my arm around his neck. "Let her go," I growl into his ear, adding a little more pressure. My forearms are bunched so tight I'm pretty sure I could keep squeezing until the guy stops breathing.

Oh, man, I'm so tempted right now.

A truck screeches to a stop on Millhouse Road and two doors open, then slam shut. Colt's running towards us with a phone pressed to his ear.

"Tyler!" Finn yells, dashing past Colt and pushing me away.

Derek sags to the ground, coughing and hacking as he struggles for air. Finn crouches down, scowling at him, looking more powerful than I've ever seen him before.

"Your parents are coming." Colt raises his chin at me, throwing Derek a dark glare before glancing at Sammy. "They were the closest."

"He's also called the police," Finn says in a deep, rumbly voice that makes Derek's bashed-up cheek fade to a ghostly pale color.

I struggle to my feet and move to Sammy's side. Crouching, I rest my hand on the side of her head as she bites her lips together and tries not to cry. She's cradling her arm again, her face almost white with pain.

"I gotta get you to the hospital." I turn to Colt and reach out my hand. "Can I borrow your truck?"

He's just digging his keys out when I hear Dad shout behind me. "Tyler!"

Running down the alley, he jolts to a stop beside us all, quickly taking in the scene, then scowling at Derek.

"Who's this guy?"

"He's the shit who hurt Sammy," I mutter.

Dad's eyebrows dip into a deep V. "You hurt my favorite teenager? Oh, we are about to have words, son."

Derek gives him a confused scowl while I fight a snicker. Sammy gives me a glassy, pained smile.

"Come on, you." I slide my arms beneath her knees and lift her up against me.

"The police are on their way," Colt's telling my dad. "We'll stay with him."

"So will I." Dad nods, then tips his head down the alley towards Fletcher Street. "Mom's got the car running. Go."

I don't hesitate. Turning the right way, I walk past my bike and head straight for Fletcher Street.

"Put me down," Sammy mumbles.

I frown at her and keep walking. "Why?"

"Because it's my *arm* that's hurting. I can still walk."

"I know." I nod.

She rolls her eyes. "Come on, Ty. This is ridiculous! I don't need to be carried like some princess!"

"I never said you did."

"Then put me down!"

Mom's car will be just around the next corner. I pick up my pace, rushing to get there before Sammy wins this fight.

"Tyler, seriously," she warns, her voice dipping low.

I jerk to a stop and glare at her for a second. She makes a move to get down but I tighten my grip. "Would you stop?"

She huffs. "Just because I'm your girlfriend now doesn't mean you have to treat me like some weak, pathetic female. I'm a tough chick."

"Yeah, you are, and I love that about you. But you also feel damn good in my arms right now and I don't want to put you down. So shut up and let me carry you, woman!"

She goes quiet, shocked still by my ranting, then lets out this adorable little snort and starts laughing. "Fine, whatever. Carry me to the car, Casanova."

"Thank you." I raise my chin like a superior gentleman and carry her to the car while she chuckles in my arms, then rests her head against my shoulder.

It feels frickin' awesome.

32

A WHOLE BUNCH OF REASONS

SAMMY

ROMA CALLS my mom on the way to the hospital. I kind of forgot she's at some ladies thing in Trentham all day.

"It's okay, Bianca. I'm happy to look after her. She can stay with us until you're done." Roma shakes her head with a smile. "It's really no trouble." She then goes quiet and glances into the backseat with a wince. "Why don't I let her tell you about it when you come to pick her up, okay?"

I grimace, then poke out my tongue when Roma hangs up the phone. "She's going to want details, isn't she?"

"Yeah, I think the dog poop's going to fly pretty far when the truth comes out."

I groan and throw my head back against Tyler's arm. "I hate the truth."

"It can be a nasty business." Roma steers the car into the hospital parking lot. She spins to look in the back, smiling at me and then winking at Tyler. "But it can also bring about awesomeness."

Her eyes shimmer with a dreamy, romantic kind of smile.

"Okay, Mom." Tyler gives her a pointed look before easing the door open.

Spinning around, he helps me out of the car, steadying me when my feet hit the asphalt. He keeps his arm on my lower back as we walk toward the massive white building.

"You're not going to carry me?" I tease.

Tyler snickers and shakes his head. "I figured you'd kick my ass if I tried to do it in public."

"Smart man," I murmur.

"Well, you love me for a reason, right?" He winks.

I grin. "A whole bunch of 'em, actually."

My words make his face kind of glow and that look holds me steady as I have to relive another examination, more X-rays, a brand new cast, plus a police interview that seems to take forever.

I beg them not to call my parents. The two officers are kind of reluctant until Roma and Donnie step up and win the awesome parents award.

"She's in our care. We're looking after her while her parents are out of town."

The police buy it without flinching, and I get away with not having to add *horrible conversation with my mother* to the list.

"You will tell them though, right?"

I nod at Roma's question but remain unsure. Mom's going to freak out. I need to make sure I explain things really carefully.

Roma takes me back to their place, and once again I'm struck by how at home I feel here. The second I walk in the door, two midget investigators return from next door, and I'm surrounded by them and a massive dog who can't get close enough to me. Laughing, I shuffle inside and plunk onto the couch. Tyler takes a seat beside me, throwing his arm over the back of the couch and snuggling in. Braxton jumps between us while Shiloh fusses with pillows, making sure my arm is resting how it should be before settling down next to her big brother. The rest of the day is spent watching the *Kung Fu Panda* trilogy.

In spite of my aching arm, I kind of float through the

day until Mom collects me at nine p.m. and I have to endure another lecture about being careful.

"You shouldn't have even been on your board."

"I wasn't—"

"I don't want to hear it! I don't even know how you got another board, but you are grounded from anything with wheels until you're out of that cast."

"But, Mom—"

"No buts! I know you're under the insane delusion that I love your sister more than you, but that's simply not the case." Mom's voice wobbles and tears pop onto her lashes. "I love you very much, and just because I don't always understand you doesn't mean I don't care deeply. I absolutely hate it when you get hurt." She flicks a quick look at me, then keeps driving. "Swollen lip and all. I know how much you love dangerous things, but it just kills me, Samantha." She sniffs. "You've always been so tough and you've never needed me the way Roxy does, but you're still my little girl. I hate the thought of you being in pain. I want my girls to be happy."

Her voice gets high and kind of screechy as she brushes the tears off her face and pulls onto our street. It's in that moment that I decide to defy Roma and stay quiet over the whole Derek thing. If she's this upset over what she assumes is a boarding accident, she'll lose it completely if she knows I was beaten up by Roxy's boyfriend. With all the other tension and angst in her life, I figure she can live without this one. I may not get away with it—who knows if the police will come knocking for more info—but if I can keep Mom out of this...I seriously think it's for the best.

She'll be absolutely mortified if she finds out what Roxy's been up to. Her precious, golden girl tarnished? That might send her over the brink.

I study her white knuckles, the strain lines on her perfectly made-up face, and decide I'll do everything I can to ease the tension thrumming inside of her.

The car jerks to a stop in our driveway and I reach for her arm.

"Mom, it really doesn't hurt that bad, but if you don't want me to skate until the cast is off then...I won't."

She gives me a weak smile and nods. "Thank you."

I'll no doubt regret saying that, but at least I have a boyfriend to entertain me when I start going stir-crazy.

Easing out of the car, I follow Mom into the house and prep myself for bumping into Roxy. I wonder what she'll have to say about Derek's Hulk act this afternoon. Surely the gossip's reached her by now.

"You hungry, sweetie?" Mom slides the purse off her shoulder and wipes the last of her tears away.

"No, I'm good. I'm just gonna go to bed."

"Okay." She nods. "If you need to take tomorrow off school, I can…"

I shake my head. "That's cool. I'm pretty sure I'll be okay."

She tips her head with an affectionate grin. "You really are a tough nugget, aren't you?"

"I kind of like that about me." I give her a tentative smile.

"I kind of like that about you, too."

Her sweet tone and the warmth in her gaze make my stomach curl with affection. "Love you, Mom."

"Ditto," she whispers. "Sleep well."

I bob my head and walk up the stairs. Roxy's light is on and her bedroom door is wide open. She's sitting on her bed, chewing gum and thumbing through some fashion magazine with a scowl on her pretty face. I bet she's pissed.

I wonder who she's more annoyed with—me for stealing her photos…or Derek for chasing me down. I swallow, remembering the spikes of fear driving through me when Derek jumped out of nowhere and tackled me to the ground, slapping my face and trying to wrench my back pocket off. His eyes were wild, glazed with a sheen of crazy...and maybe a little fear. Is that what drove him? The fear of getting busted?

Roxy catches me looking in as I come up the stairwell. Her head jolts back, her scowl changing from anger to confusion.

"What happened to you?"

I pause, resting my good hand on the banister, not sure what to say. She looks like she doesn't know. Is this an act?

"Um." I scratch my forehead, going for vague. "I had a fall."

She rolls her eyes. "You're such an idiot. Was a broken arm not enough? You have to break your face too? When are you going to give up skating already?"

I stare at her, studying every facet of her expression. She seriously looks genuine right now.

With a cool shrug, I climb the stairs, then rest my butt against the railing outside her door. "So, what did you do today?"

She gives me a *like you care* kind of look before continuing to thumb through her magazine. "I just hung out here."

"Did...Michelle come over?"

"No." Roxy scowls and chews her gum a little harder. "I spent the day *alone*...plotting my revenge."

The antagonistic glint in her eye doesn't match the sharpness of her words. The way she's snapping at me gives away just how annoyed she is. Oh, man, does she think Derek ditched her after their shower?

I look for her phone, surprised he hasn't texted her with the details.

Then again, hardly details the guy would want to share.

Oh yeah, hey baby, so I caught your sister with the memory card and went ape-shit. She hit me in the face with her cast then I got into a fight with your prom date and now I'm spending the day at the police station. I could be looking at jail time if I don't get my shit together. Love you, my evil little girlfriend.

"What are you staring at?" Roxy's sharp voice jolts me upright, her annoyance no doubt amplified by the fact I didn't rise to her revenge quip.

"Nothing," I mumble and turn for my room.

The pages of Roxy's magazine flick back with quick snaps, giving away how pissed off she is. I walk through my bedroom door in a kind of daze. My brain's muddled right now, but there's this idea dancing around in the background that I can't ignore. I want to give Roxy the benefit of the doubt. I want to assume that she's been seeing Derek on the side, that he was the one who stole her camera and he persuaded someone else to take those photos of Layla...but that won't change the fact that Roxy did still out Kaija. I have Dana's word, and I believe it.

Tyler brought me in on this thing to protect Layla. We've got the photos now and Derek's in for it, but Roxy is still an unknown. We have to find out one way or another how much of a part she had to play in this whole thing. And we have to get that information in a way that will protect us all.

Closing the door behind me, I hurry to my bed and yank out my phone.

I start with Mack.

He answers after only one ring. "Hey, you okay? I just spoke to Tyler."

"Yeah. I'm fine."

"I knew something was up. When Kaija and I got back from the lake, Martin was fuming. He left the house shouting something about idiot children." Mack's laughter is more like a bark then a genuine chuckle. "What'd Roxy say?"

"That's the thing. I don't think she knows what went down."

Mack goes silent for a long, slow beat. "How is that even possible?"

"I have no idea, but I think we should take advantage of it."

"How do you mean?"

I purse my lips and lie back to gaze up at my extreme sports posters. "You know how you pranked Kaija with that spider last year?"

"Yeah…" he answers slowly.

"How'd you get into her locker?"

"Why? What are you thinking?"

I tell him.

33

AN APOLOGY LONG OVERDUE

TYLER

SAMMY'S IDEA is freaking brilliant.

Mack called me just after ten and I gave up on the idea of sleeping and got straight to work. Dad was still up when I popped down to the kitchen, and I updated him in a way that would put Tori's speed-talking to shame. I mean, I gave him everything from the Kaija crisis to breaking into Derek's house to realizing I was in love with Sammy.

Somehow he managed to keep up with it all, his facial expression covering a range of emotions as he listened. By the time I was done, he looked spent, and all he could do was mumble, "Geez, Ty, I thought my high school days were exciting. They were nothing compared to this."

"I'd hardly say exciting, Dad. It's kind of been a nightmare."

He nods and gives me a lopsided grin. "Except for the part where you've woken up and realized how awesome my favorite teenager is."

I roll my eyes. "You know I'm a teenager too, right?"

"Yeah." He shrugs. "But she's still my favorite." I give his arm a light punch and his smile cracks immediately. With a rough chuckle, he pulls me into a tight hug. "I love you, kid."

"Love you too, Dad." Slapping him on the back, I pull away and rest against the kitchen counter. "So, what do you think? Is it gonna work?"

"It's a solid plan and you're welcome to use my stuff. Come on, I'll show you how to set it up." With a flick of his hand, he leads me down to his office and then proves Sammy's theory right: Donnie Schumann really is the best dad in the world.

———

I rest my foot on the backseat of Mack's Camaro, keeping an eye out for Sam. It's like six in the morning and we're heading in to school. No one in the car can talk as we nervously wait for our plan to fall into place.

Dad's equipment is in the trunk. Mack's all set to

sweet-talk the janitor, and all we can hope for now is that Roxy will fall into our trap.

"Here she comes," Mack murmurs, then frowns as he leans closer to the rearview mirror. "What the f—?"

Kaija's door snaps open and she jumps out before he can even finish.

"What are you doing here?" Her voice is sharp and edgy, making me spin to find out what the hell is going on.

My chest restricts as soon as I spot a pale Dana Foster quivering beside Sammy.

"Give her a break, she wanted to come."

Kaija glares at Sammy. "Why?"

I wrestle with the latch and push the seat forward so I can get out and stand beside my girlfriend. I don't know why the hell she decided to bring the freshman, but I want to back her up either way.

Dana wrings her hands and looks up to Sammy. With a little nudge, Sam urges her to say whatever it is they obviously rehearsed beforehand.

"Okay, um…" Dana tucks a curl behind her ear, her eyes already shimmering with tears. "Sammy texted me last night to say that you found out what I did and I

begged her to let me come this morning so I could..."
She lets out a shaky breath.

I sidle up behind Sammy, running my hand down her
back while keeping an eye on Kaija's face. Her green
eyes are stormy, her body language confronting—
crossed arms, bunched lips, flaring nostrils.

"It's okay," Sammy whispers. "Just say it."

"I'm sorry," Dana blurts. "I was an idiot to let her up
to your room. I shouldn't have cared about being cool
or trying to impress her. I didn't know what she would
do with your diary, and I swear I didn't see what she
saw. As I was handing it over, I kind of felt like it was
wrong, but I was so nervous having her in the house I
could barely string two sentences together, let alone
think straight enough to figure out she was up to no
good." Her lips tremble and she starts blinking,
setting a couple of tears free. "When I saw those
pictures and read the story, I just..." Dana shakes her
head. "At first, I thought she just made it up, but
then..."

Kaija swallows, her cheeks flaring with color as she
looks to the ground. Her quivering jaw works to the
side and when Mack puts his arm around her she looks
up with glassy eyes. Her lips bunch into a tortured
frown and Mack kisses the side of her head. "It's okay,
Kiwi. It's in the past."

Kaija sniffs and nods, pressing the back of her hand against her mouth.

"I've avoided her since," Dana whispers.

"Only because she threatened you," Mack mutters, his dark glare enough to disintegrate the terrified freshman.

She shrinks away from it but shakes her head. "That's not the only reason. What she did was wrong, and I lost complete respect for her. I avoid her now because I realize she's not a nice person and I don't want to be like her." Unzipping her bag, Dana tugs out a sheet of paper and holds it out to Kaija. "I want to help you guys end this."

Taking the sheet, Kaija scans the contents, her lips rising into a slow half-smile. With a quick nod, she looks down at Dana and sighs. "Okay, you big idiot, you're in."

Dana responds with a nervous grin.

Looking at the sheet again, Kaija purses her lips before giving Dana a proper, heart-felt smile. "Thanks for this."

"You didn't deserve what she did to you. Even if that cartoon was true, you're a good person. You made a mistake and from what Sammy's told me, you fixed it."

"I did." Kaija nods. "But it still hurts sometimes."

"Yeah, well, that's what makes you decent." Dana hitches her bag onto her shoulder. "That's what makes me want to be like you instead of her."

Kaija and Sammy snicker in unison.

Dana looks between them. "What?"

Sammy shakes her head with a grin. "How about you just start by being you and see how you go with that."

Dana's cheeks fire red and then she lets out this nervous titter that turns into a giggle.

"Okay." I bulge my eyes at Mack and tip my chin at his car. "Let's go."

He nods and we squeeze into his car. Sammy sits on my knee and we hope we don't get busted as we haul ass to school in time to set everything up before Roxy and Layla arrive.

34

THE DOWNFALL OF ROXANNE CARMICHAEL

SAMMY

MY STOMACH JUMPS and jitters as I hover beside Tyler, looking over his shoulder at the iPad in his hands.

Colt glances at him. "You sure this is going to work?"

Tyler just gives him a look—*come on, man, of course it is.*

My lips twitch with a smile, proud of Tyler's ability with technical stuff. He's always been into it...just like his dad. Donnie is freaking epic to let us borrow some of his security stuff. I shake my head, still amazed by how different our parents are. He told them everything about what went down with Layla, Derek, Roxy—the whole shebang. Well, he told his dad and his dad told his mom. Apparently, they both took it cool as cucumbers, then agreed with Tyler that my idea was awesome.

Crazy grown-ups.

I love them!

"Okay, she's coming." Mack ducks around the corner, throwing his arm over Kaija's shoulders and pulling her close. His lips press against her hair as we listen to the sound of Roxy and Layla approaching.

"I don't know why you needed picking up so early this morning," Roxy grumbles.

"Wow," I whisper. "The mic's picking her up already."

Tyler winks at me and we all hold our breath as we wait for Roxy to fling open her locker and give us everything we need.

"Sorry," Layla says. "It's just Mack's busy with Kaija today and I have some homework to finish up. I always do better in the library. There are too many distractions at home."

"Yeah, yeah, whatever." Roxy flicks her locker open, giving us the perfect view of her face. "I'm the world's best friend…" Her voice peters off as she spies the little gift we left in her locker.

"You are." Layla's tone is so sweet it's almost hard to catch how bogus it is. The second Mack told her about my plan, she jumped all over it. I guess her shock has given way to anger after all.

The locker beside Roxy's creaks. I'm assuming Layla is leaning against it while Roxy glares at the piece of paper in her hand.

"What have you got there?" Layla asks, still pulling off the perfect performance.

"Someone's making up shit about me," Roxy mutters. "They're trying to hurt me, just like they hurt Kaija."

"What?" Layla comes into view over Roxy's shoulder. "What do you mean?"

"Nothing," Roxy seethes. The sound of scrunching paper disrupts the mic.

"Let me see."

"No!" Roxy snaps.

Layla's head tips to the side, giving us a decent shot of her face. "Why not?"

Roxy eyes bulge, then close. She has no idea there's a tiny camera in the corner of her locker, giving us everything. After a pause, she opens her eyes and puts on one of her plastic expressions before spinning to speak to Layla.

"It's just some dumb cartoon trying to say I stole Kaija's diary." She shakes her head. "As if I would."

I can't see what's happening, but I'm assuming Layla is taking the sheet of paper and smoothing it out. That's what it sounds like.

"Wow," she murmurs, this time not really hiding her horror. If anything, she sounds deadpan.

I wince, hoping she doesn't give herself away as she looks at the stick-figure depictions of Roxy sneaking into Kaija's room and taking photos of her diary, then drawing up pictures and plastering them on the school walls.

"Whoever the hell drew that is going down," Roxy fumes.

"I did." Dana's voice comes clearly through the mic.

I hold my breath, knowing how nervous she is. Her voice is quivering slightly as she walks into view. I can see the side of her face next to Layla.

"Excuse me?" Roxy's icy tone could freeze the Atlantic.

Dana swallows and looks at Layla, who's still trying to play Roxy's best friend and isn't much help just yet.

"Come on, Dana," I murmur. "Don't run scared."

Clearing her throat, she flicks a curl off her cheek and repeats, "I did. I drew it."

There's a cold, drawn-out pause that makes me hold my breath. Nibbling on the edge of my thumbnail, I watch intensely, half expecting to have to run down the hallway and rescue Dana from Roxy's hands around her throat.

Thankfully, my sister keeps her talons retracted and just goes for a venomous tone that makes my skin crawl.

"What the hell were you hoping to achieve by this?"

Dana flinches as Roxy moves forward, blocking the timid freshman from view.

"Is this some kind of threat?"

"No," Dana murmurs. "It's just the truth."

Roxy snatches the sheet out of Layla's hands and starts ripping it up. "Whose truth? Like anyone is going to believe a pathetic, useless nobody over me."

"My turn," Kaija whispers, stepping out of Mack's embrace and walking out from our hiding spot. "I will. I'll believe her." Her voice stretches down the hallway, making Layla bite back a smile and Roxy groan.

"Ugh. Would you just go home already?"

"Aw, don't you worry your pretty little head, Roxanne. I'm leaving soon. But I couldn't fly away without giving you this." She holds out another sheet of paper—stick figure drawings of her getting it on with Derek Wiseman. The speech bubbles have them plotting how to set Layla up at the party.

"What the hell is this?" Roxy shouts.

"Would you just stop?" Kaija counters with the same tone and volume. "We all know what you did to me... and your best friend, Layla. You can't act your way out of this, Roxanne Carmichael. It's time for you to go down, you conniving little bitch."

"How dare you speak to me that way? I've done nothing! I don't even know what photos you've tried to depict in these shitty drawings!" We catch a glimpse of Kaija's cartoon as Roxy waves it in the air.

"I can help with that." Layla looks down and pulls something out of her bag while she's talking. "I think she's referring to these ones."

Oh man, I wish I could see Roxy's face right now. A tendon in her neck is straining and she's barely moving as Layla holds out the pictures. The best friend play is over. I glimpse Layla's expression over Roxy's shoulder and can clearly see her rage. It's that silent, intimidating kind that makes you want to shrink into a corner.

Roxy's blouse rustles as she crosses her arms and pulls her shoulders back, refusing to take the images.

"Here, let me show you." Layla holds them up and

starts flicking through them. We catch glimpses of the shots as they flash past the video camera.

I glance over at Finn. His jaw is locked tight as he scowls at the screen. I think those images will forever hurt him. I can't wait to be done with this so we can burn them for good.

Roxy turns away from the images, staring into her locker with a panicked look on her face. Her eyes dart from side to side as she starts blinking like crazy. "Gross, Layla," she huffs, but her voice is shaking. "I don't know how you could let those assholes touch you. I thought you hated your stepbrother."

"Oh, I do. More than I can ever express in words, but what kills me even more is that my best friend went behind my back and allowed her creepy boyfriend to touch me. You got me wasted and you put me in this position. You promised to protect me and threw me into a lion's den!" Layla's voice pitches with emotion. I can't see her face anymore but I don't need to; it's all there in her tone, in the way the words shakily tumble out of her mouth.

Roxy pales, her lips trembling as she tries to bunch them together. "I did no such thing." She grits out the words, then spins. "I would never do something so disgusting. And I would never date that creep! Your cartoon is bullshit, and these pictures are fake! You're just trying to set me up! Ganging up on me! Now that you've got new friends you don't need me anymore. You—"

"Cut the bullshit, you pathetic drama queen," Kaija cuts her off. "We got these images off your camera!"

"My cue." I give Tyler an edgy grin. He squeezes my hand, then lets go so I can dash down the hallway.

"My camera?" Roxy snaps. "I haven't used my camera in months."

I pull up to my sister's side and hold out the camera I took from her desk while she was in the bathroom this morning. "That's a total lie, Roxy, and you know it. Time to give up the goods."

She snatches the camera out of my hand and yells, "You stole my camera? Mom is so hearing about this!"

"Yeah, after I tell her about the photos I found on there."

Roxy gives me a smug smirk. "You don't have shit. There is no proof those photos came from my camera."

"You sure about that, Roxy?" I cross my arms. "Or did you not check the bottom drawer of your jewelry box this morning?"

Her lips flatline, her eyes trying to slice me in half as she recovers and goes for yet another lie. "I don't know what you're talking ab—"

"Yes, you do!" I snap, pointing at the images in Layla's hand, then at the ripped-up cartoons on the floor. Yanking my own drawing from my back pocket, I unfold it and show her my stick figure depictions of her snappy happy at the party, setting Layla up.

With a growl, Roxy tears the sheet from my hand and rips it to shreds.

"You can't prove anything." Roxy turns her camera over, flicking open the bottom and pulling out a memory card. "There's nothing on here."

"Probably not, but the one I took from your room yesterday is loaded with evidence."

"Oh, really?" Roxy's voice is high and cynical as she tries to counter my attack. "And where is that?"

"With the police." Layla's voice is low with warning. "Along with my statement."

"And mine," I add quietly.

Roxy flashes me a dark look. As much as it chills me, I press on. "Derek was in our house yesterday. He chased me down and hurt me."

She blinks and clenches her jaw, her nostrils flaring. "That's not true. You had a skating accident."

I shake my head but she yells over my silent denial.

"He's on probation. Like he would risk even coming to Nelson."

I step into her space. "He has a temper."

"He's not stupid!"

"Oh, yeah? Then where was he when you got out of the shower yesterday afternoon? Didn't you wonder why he just split without even saying goodbye?"

"It's called self-preservation! He can't afford to get caught. I don't question his every move!" she practically screams, then stops short, her skin blanching as she spins back to her locker. If only she knew we were catching everything on her face right now. I bet she's blinking. She does that when she knows she's busted.

"Why are you defending that asshole?" Layla whispers. "How could you...even be with him?"

I stare at Roxy's profile. Her nostrils are still flaring, her mouth dipping into an ugly line as she grips the metal door. "You all think you're so perfect with your hot boyfriends," she seethes. "But you're nothing more than a slut, a bully, and a she-man!" She spins around, her icy-blue eyes filled with hatred as she points at Kaija. "Mack was supposed to be mine! You had no right coming in here and taking him from me. I did what I had to do. So don't go judging me. You can speculate all you like, but I'm going to deny everything."

Layla and Dana shrink back from Roxy's venom but Kaija and I both rise against it, pulling up to our full heights as we glare at her.

"Bummer for you that Derek didn't say the same thing." I don't actually know if that's true, but we're trying to rattle the truth out of my sister and I'm doing everything I can to get the entire story.

Kaija looks down at her nails, mimicking Roxy's aloof eyebrow raise perfectly.

"But like you pointed out, self-preservation, right? If he can't afford to get caught, then he's probably going to dump you in it to protect his own ass."

Roxy's skin drains of color. I actually have a flash of pity for her. She looks ready to dissolve as she gapes at each of us, her cool veneer slipping for a moment.

But not for long.

Her upper lip soon curls as she slams her locker closed and stalks down the hall, her boot heels smacking against the hard tiles.

Too bad for her she's about to round the corner and bump straight into a bunch of riled boyfriends.

35

THE CHEESE PUFF EVASION

TYLER

WE LOST sight of Roxy the second her locker slammed shut, but we hear her coming. Oh, man, do we hear her coming!

She screams around the corner, nearly barreling into Mack. He stands tall when she bumps into his chest then takes a quick step back.

"What the hell are you guys doing? Get out of my way!"

I answer her question by raising the iPad and running my finger over the bottom bar. I rewind back to the look on her face as she's reading Dana's cartoon.

She watches in stunned silence, her cheeks flaming red while her bright eyes swirl a dark blue. We get up to the part where Layla's walking her through the party betrayal and Roxy's face blanches as she gapes at the screen and sees just how much she's given away.

I glare at her. "Weird how the face can sometimes be louder than the mouth."

"You can deny as much as you like, Rox, but we all know the truth now." Colt crosses his arms, looking just a little smug. Tori mimics his pose and expression. If I weren't so riled at Roxy right now, I'd probably laugh. Pixie Girl's cute when she's trying to be tough.

"And if you ever use it against our girls again, it's going to come back and annihilate you." Finn's deep voice makes her shrink back, her eyes skimming his dark brown glare before jumping over to the guy she wanted from the start.

She gives him a pleading look, but it only makes his expression harder.

"You got that?" He raises his eyebrows and all that's left for her to do is duck around him and stalk away.

I turn to watch her, just like I used to. Her hips are swaying with that usual confident strut. She clips towards the front entrance just as a wave of students walks into the school. Raising her chin, she pulls back her shoulders and muscles her way through them. In true Roxy style, she's going to keep her dignity firmly intact. It's the thing she treasures most, and I'm pretty confident she's not going to risk her rep by letting us expose her.

"Man, thank God this year's nearly over." Mack runs his hands through his hair, letting out a heavy sigh.

The girls appear behind him, Kaija's arms snaking around his waist. She props her chin on his shoulder and smiles. "What are you talking about? This has been the best year ever."

He gives her a weird frown while Layla giggles and rises on her toes to kiss Finn. "I agree." She nestles her head into his chest. "It may have been full of a lot of shit, but it's also been filled with truth...and it's brought us together."

Sammy rests her arm on my shoulder and whispers, "Yeah, this is starting to get a little too corny, don't you think? Quick, make a joke before Tori starts talking as we all turn into cheese puffs."

I turn and look straight into those stunning blue eyes of hers, desperately trying to resist the urge to go a little cheesy myself. She's going to make it damn hard on me.

With a short snicker, I wink and start speaking just as Tori opens her mouth. "Well, as much as I'd love to stand around spouting sentiments and watching you loved-up freaks get your kissy faces on, I'm gonna take my girl here and go make out with her in the back corner of the library."

Sammy's cheeks flare red and she punches me with her left fist. "I said a joke, not a..." She shakes her head and sighs while everyone in the group starts laughing.

"Hey, I made them laugh, didn't I? Cheese puffs averted."

Sammy snorts and takes over the laughter while everyone else looks at us like we're weird.

I wink at her and she gives me the kind of smile that says everything she needs to without opening her mouth. Nudging her arm off my shoulder, I pull her against me and nibble her neck. She snickers and twitches, laughing when I hit her ticklish spot.

I'm sure she'll get me back later, and I kinda can't wait. The first bell rings, telling us it's time to get our shit together. Everyone says goodbye and I grab Sammy's hand, threading my fingers between hers and ignoring the trail of surprised whispers that follow us to our lockers.

As much as I hate gossip, I accept that it's a part of school life. Besides, I may not want them spreading nasty rumors about Layla, but they can gossip all they like about me falling for my best friend.

36

TRUTH IS A NASTY BUSINESS

SAMMY

SO ROXY NEVER CAME BACK TO school. I'm not completely surprised, but maybe mildly. It's unlike her to let something beat her. I mean, we got her good and she knows she can't mess with us anymore, but still. I was expecting her to strut into the cafeteria at lunchtime and when she didn't, it got me wondering.

The whole flesh-and-blood thing...I've been struggling with it. I know this because when I walk into my house after school and I hear her crying upstairs, my heart does this strange little tug.

"Your sister's got her period. Really bad cramps, poor darling," Mom explains as she walks past with a hamper full of laundry. "I've given her some meds. Hopefully, she'll pick up soon."

My forehead wrinkles with a skeptical frown but Mom's already through the kitchen, oblivious to my cynicism. Probably a good thing.

"Hey, Sammy," Dad calls from the dining room. I pop my head in, figuring out why Mom raced away from me so fast.

I give him a tight smile. "Hey, Dad."

He glances up from his computer and rolls his eyes at me. "Might want to avoid the pink cave this afternoon."

He winks and all I can do is snicker and murmur, "Thanks for the advice."

He doesn't hear me, his eyes already back on the screen.

Nipping the corner of my lip, I gaze up the stairs, then turn to look at the front door. I'm tempted to split and head straight to Tyler's place. But then I hear Roxy whimper again and I can't go yet.

With a heavy sigh, I start trudging up the stairs. Part of me wants to ignore my sister. It's a two-fold thing, really. For one, she's a total bitch. I think of everything she's done this year to hurt people and shake my head as I stand at the top of the stairwell. It's totally crazy.

But...

I set her up today. I threw her into a boiling vat of

disclosure. I made her cry, and although she might deserve it, I'm not ready to ignore her until I find out exactly why she let all this shit go down.

I knock on her door and push it open, even when she tells me to get lost.

Leaning against the doorframe, I take in her blotchy red face and puffy eyelids. Her eyes are a vibrant blue, the tears making them gleam.

"You okay?"

"Does it look like I'm okay?" she snaps, snatching a tissue and dabbing her face before throwing it onto the mounting pile at the foot of her bed. "Thanks for every-thing today, Sam. You're such a great sister."

I counter her sarcasm with an eye roll. "You deserved it, Rox, and you know it." Stepping into her room, I swing the door shut behind me and perch on the edge of her desk. "We could have been a lot meaner. You have no idea how tempting it is to bury you. Kaija and Mack want to take the video straight to the police, but Layla of all people...the one who should be broad-casting that shit to the world says we should keep it for insurance only." I couldn't believe it when she first said it, but I'm wondering if she's protecting herself as well. If we expose Roxy, the chances of those ugly photos flying free will be pretty damn high as well. I clear my throat to ward off the sickening chill I get every time I remember those photos. "If you don't do anything crazy, we'll never need to use it, and as tempted as I am, I won't tell Mom about any of this." I point at her. "Unless you try to hurt me or Tyler, or any of my friends."

"Like I'm worried about Mom. I can get around her any day of the week," Roxy scoffs. "But I needed insurance of my own. What do you think the photos of Layla were?" she snaps. "Derek was not supposed to use them that way. No one was ever supposed to see them, but I was worried she'd figure it all out and I needed a backup plan."

I gape at her, flicking my arms wide. "Layla's your best friend. How could you set her up like that? It's so obvious she wasn't into it, but you just kept clicking?"

"The stuff I put in her drink was supposed to make her forget everything. If Derek hadn't pulled that dick move while I was in LA, it would have been fine."

"You just don't get it!" My voice pitches high.

"What!" She scowls at me. "It wasn't even a full roofie. We used like half a pill. Derek sourced it from some guys at his school who said it was mild shit. They assured him it wouldn't be harmful."

"Are you kidding me? Not harmful!"

"I mean like physically. It wasn't going to kill her or

anything—it was just going to make her a little...uninhibited. She wasn't supposed to find out about it, so no harm, no foul, right?"

"No! Not right!" I screech. "You set her up with her creepy stepbrother and took photos! Gross, Roxy! People go to prison for that kind of shit!"

"Yeah, well, no one was supposed to know about it!"

"Oh, well that makes it better!" My tone is sharp and cutting.

She rolls her eyes at me, letting out a tired sigh. Turning away, she stares at the window, then starts to blink. "Did Derek really hurt you yesterday?"

The quiet way she says it makes me wonder if she actually cares. I shrug and go for blasé. "Tyler got there to help me out. It wasn't too bad."

"He promised me he wouldn't touch anyone else," she whispers. "I was so mad at him when he went after Finn and Layla at the lake. I tried to break up with him after that, but he swore he didn't know what came over him." She tuts and shakes her head. "He seemed so sincere."

I have to admit I'm kind of horrified right now. It's so incredibly obvious how much she cares for that dickwad. "Are you seriously in love with Derek Wiseman? I thought you still had a thing for Mack?"

She lets out a bitter scoff. "I did have a thing for Mack, but that died pretty quickly when I realized what a blind idiot he was. Going after Kaija like that?" Her upper lip curls as she shakes her head.

"So why torture them that way? Why make such a big song and dance at school about Mack being yours?"

Her icy glare hits me like a laser beam. "Because he *should* have been mine. You honestly think I'm going to let myself get beaten by some murdering little slut?"

The words make me shudder, especially the way she says them with this malicious smile on her face.

"You are one twisted little freak." I wrinkle my nose. "No wonder you and Derek got together. You're perfect for each other."

Her dark smile flashes with sadness. She pulls her knees to her chest and rocks back against her pillows. "When we first met, it was like…addictive." Her blue eyes skim mine then dip to her nails. She rubs her thumb over the shiny polish, her voice taking on a soft, dream-like timbre. "There was something about him that I just couldn't resist. I went over to see Layla to try to smooth things over after our fight. When he opened the door, our eyes met and there was this intense attraction between us. We were up in his room naked before I even realized what I was doing."

I make a disgusted face.

"Don't look at me like that. He's a great kisser, and really good with his hands." She looks to the ceiling and swallows. "And he knew just what to say. In spite of everything Layla had told me, I liked him. For some reason, it was just so easy to let him in on everything. It wasn't until I was driving home later that I realized how much Layla would hate me if she found out. When I told Derek I was worried she'd work out I was the cartoon culprit or figure out we were sleeping together, he told me I just needed a little insurance policy." She sucks in a ragged breath. "The original idea was just to take pics of Quaid and Layla getting it on, but then on the night..." Her voice trailed off. "I should have hated him for jumping in on the action, but it only made the photos more powerful and user-friendly. They would shut Layla up if she ever did discover what I'd done."

"Why did you think she'd work it out? We live in the same house and I had no idea."

"Gimme a break. We barely speak to each other! Layla and I do everything together, and she noticed that Dana was acting edgy. And then she started having these fuzzy memories about the New Year's Eve party. She actually accused me of being the one who outed Kaija, and I knew I couldn't just sit back and do nothing. I had to act before she got too close." Roxy bites her lips together. "I swear, Derek never told me he was going to use those photos to blackmail her. But he's kind of persuasive, you know? When I tried to dump him, I just… Layla had Finn and she was busy being friends with Tori! Mack's totally whipped and I… I missed Derek, okay?" She flicks her hands up, her knees flopping on to the bed. Picking at the duvet cover, she mumbles, "I went to visit him in Brownridge and we just kind of got back together. I didn't expect anyone to find out, and the only reason I kept those photos was to cover myself in case Derek turned on me. I knew I was playing with fire, but I just couldn't help it."

I grip the edge of her desk as I take in her raw confession. I know it's honest because I've never seen Roxy look like this before.

"I didn't expect anyone to ever find them. I didn't think you'd have the guts to go into my room and look for my camera. After I caught you outside my door that day, I even played it extra safe and moved the memory card into my jewelry box, the last place you would ever try and go."

I sigh and cross my ankles. "Initially, I just wanted to borrow it so I could get in good with some of the photography kids at school. Tyler and I were trying to hunt down the party paparazzo. I never thought it'd be my own sister," I finish with a whisper.

Roxy purses her lips, refusing to make eye contact with me.

I stare at the top of her head, still trying to figure out

how I feel about her. It's kind of hard to move past totally disgusted. How can I be related to this person?

"What are you going to do now?"

She looks up, her lips dipping into a sad frown while her eyes glass with tears. "I've broken up with him."

"Do you think he'll try to get together with you again?"

She shrugs and sniffs. "I don't know."

"Do you think you'll be able to resist him?"

She lets out a scoffing breath and blinks at the window again. "Do you know what it's like to feel addicted to someone?"

"Yes." I nod, surprised by how fast my answer comes.

Roxy looks at me, kind of skeptical.

I can't help the soft smile cresting over my lips. "I guess I just got lucky that the someone I can't get enough of happens to be a really good guy...and my best friend."

Her perfect nose wrinkles, but then her lips dip again and she lets out a dry snigger. "It must have killed you when he went to prom with me."

"Well, you did say you were trying to piss me off."

"I thought it'd work better than it did. I guess I underestimated you." Her tone is biting again, her bright eyes glittering.

I run my finger over my cast and admit, "Actually, it worked pretty damn well. Watching you make out with him and steal him away from me...it pissed me off real good. It kinda hurt too."

Her lips twitch with a fleeting smile.

I frown. "Why? Why did that make you smile?"

She shrugs. "Because I get a sick sense of satisfaction watching other people suffer."

My face bunches with disbelief.

"You want the truth, little sister? Well, there it is. Watching others being pulled down makes me feel better about myself." Her superior confidence slips for a second and I catch a glimpse of her haunted gaze as she mutters, "That's probably why I was attracted to such an asshole. You're right, he is the perfect match for me."

"You don't have to stay that way, you know."

"I don't know how to be anything else! I don't even know why I'm like it in the first place. I just am."

"I'll help you. What do you need? We can do this one step at a time. You could start by saying sorry to Layla."

I don't even know why I'm offering to do this. Maybe

it's a desperate need for my sister to redeem herself. To finally be related to someone I can be proud to introduce as family.

Roxy shoots me down with a dry glare. "Not gonna happen. I don't even know how to say that word without looking like a complete idiot."

"Humility doesn't make you look like an idiot. If you don't make this right, you're going to end this school year with no friends."

She raises her chin. "At least I'll have my dignity."

"A pretty lonely companion, if you ask me."

She sniffs and looks away, her lips wobbling as she presses them together.

"You know, you look like Mom when you make that face."

Roxy flinches, but keeps her gaze out the window. I stand from the desk, catching a movement out of the corner of my eye. Roxy can't see it from where she's sitting on the bed, but her entire day is about to end even worse than the way it started.

I gaze down at the officers in blue. One of them hitches his belt while the other pulls out a notepad as they stroll up to our front door.

I press my lips together, resisting the urge to warn her.

I don't know why. I guess I just want to see her face when she figures out they're probably here to talk to her.

Walking across the room, I open her door just as the doorbell rings. She scowls at me.

"Is that your best-buddy boyfriend? Here to whisk you away on his beat-up skateboard?" Her scathing tone is knocked dead when a deep voice travels up to us.

"Afternoon, ma'am. We're Officers King and Stilman. Are you Mrs. Carmichael?"

"Yes." Mom's reply is slow and cautious.

"We'd like to speak to your daughter, please."

Roxy's mouth dips with fear, her milky skin paling.

Mom mutters something I can't decipher, then calls up the stairs. "Samantha!"

"Actually, ma'am, we're here to see Roxanne Carmichael."

Everything freezes for a second. I grip the door handle. Breaths start punching out of Roxy's chest, fast and erratic. The next sound we hear is the scraping of Dad's chair followed by my mother's weak tremor.

"Why? Why do you need to speak with her?"

"We're investigating an incident involving party drugs,

and we have reason to believe your daughter's involved."

"She was roofied?" my dad thunders, his voice booming up the stairs.

"No, sir." The officer's voice remains cool and even. "We have a witness account saying she supplied the drugs and went on to take photos of her friend in a very compromising position. I'm sure she's aware that party drugs and unsolicited sexual acts are illegal. We need to ask her a few questions and take a statement."

Roxy closes her eyes, cursing Derek under her breath.

"Feeling better about yourself now, sis?"

Her eyes snap open and she tries to take me down with a venomous glare. All I can do is smirk at it. "It's called comeuppance. And it's about damn time you got yours. So don't bother lying. We've got video footage that can bury you. This is your chance to do the right thing and not make it worse for yourself."

Her glare is getting blacker by the second.

With a soft snicker, I shake my head. "Every choice has consequences. Isn't that what you and Mom always say?"

She flips me off, her upper lip curling. "Get out."

I purse my lips, raise my eyebrows, and quietly leave her room.

"Roxanne!" Dad calls from the bottom of the stairs. "Get down here, right now!"

I head to my room, not willing to turn back and see Roxy shuffle down the stairs. My conversation with her, although fully enlightening, drenches me in this overwhelming sadness. No wonder I never feel at home in this house. I'm living with people determined to self-destruct—a sister who likes to hurt her friends, a father obsessed with work or weekend sports, and a mother who can't face it all so she puts on a sunny veneer to hide her pain.

With a heavy sigh, I abandon the whole *spending the evening in my room* idea and go to my window instead. I should probably stick around and eavesdrop on Roxy's nightmare, but I'm pretty sure that's just going to depress me. I'll find out the truth about what she said when I get back. I'm sure the house will be icy cool either way, and I have no doubts that Dad will tell me everything. The guy likes to rant when he's pissed off.

Pulling the window open, I squeeze through the space and onto the roof, then carefully make my way to the drainpipe. I've done it plenty of times before and shimmy down with ease, even with a broken arm.

As soon as my feet hit the path, I brush my hands off

on the back of my ripped-up jeans and start heading for the best place in Nelson.

I don't feel like staying home tonight, not when I could be dining in a crazy, loud, happy house where laughter is king and honesty is something to aspire to.

37

FOUND THE PERFECT START

TYLER

SO ROXY TOLD THE TRUTH. It was a miracle none of us were expecting. I had the video all ready to hand over to the police, but in the end I didn't have to.

Sammy called me as soon as she got back to her house and told me Roxy had given her statement, putting Derek and Quaid in serious hot water and her on probation. The day after graduation, she fled Nelson and is currently under the watchful eye of her Aunt Trudy. No, not the totally chic one who owns the boutique fashion shop in Portland but the one who lives on a cattle ranch in Montana. If Roxy's well behaved and works hard, then she's allowed to transfer to Portland after Christmas, but I don't envy her the summer she's in for.

I can't help snickering every time I think of it. When I compare it to the summer my friends and I have planned, Roxy's the biggest loser of us all.

And that's just the way it should be.

Summer.

Bring it on.

Except for this part...

I gaze around the airport and try to muster a smile, but Mack's making it really hard on all of us.

Trentham Airport is crowded as families leave on their different summer vacations. We stand in a slightly somber circle, getting ready to say goodbye to the guy we've all looked up to for years.

"Come on, you guys." Mack slaps me on the arm. "It's not like we can't still Skype...Facetime...Snapchat... Tweet! The possibilities are endless."

His chipper tone and lame attempt at humor fall flat.

Instead, we all just nod, but can't quite say anything. It's been a bittersweet week. Amy Briggs—Tori's best friend and this year's valedictorian—gave an epic graduation speech about saying goodbye and moving onto bigger things. It was totally depressing. I'm not ready to say goodbye to Mack...or Colt, and okay, even Tori. The chick's seriously grown on me. I know they'll only be a few hours away, but it won't change the fact that the next time I stroll into Nelson High I won't see Mack's orange and blue Camaro in the lot. Finn's head won't be bobbing above everyone else's as we walk the halls. Colt won't be standing back field with me, ready to run the play.

"Flight UA5357 to LA is now boarding." The intercom's message makes instant tears pop onto Layla's lashes.

Pursing my lips, I try not to let my angst show. I should be happy for the guy. He's pursuing his dreams...just like Amy told us to.

Finn wraps his arm around Layla, pulling her against his chest. She leans in to him, sniffing while she watches her mom and Martin say their goodbyes. He then steps away from them and starts his round with us.

I'm first.

Grabbing his hand, I pull him into my chest and slap him on the back.

"Gonna miss you, man," Mack murmurs.

I step back and lightly punch his shoulder. "Yeah, I guess I'll miss you too."

We just stare at each other for a second and say it all without talking.

He grins and bobs his head before giving Sammy a quick hug. "Take care of him for me."

"You know I will," she whispers, looking way more serious than I'm used to.

Stepping out of his embrace, she crosses her arms and shuffles over to me. I untuck her hand from beneath her arm and thread our fingers together.

She gives me a sad smile and rests her head on my shoulder. Mack hugs each one of us, then collects up his bag and grins.

"I love you guys." He swallows, then looks to his mom. "I'll call you when I get there, okay?"

"Okay, sweetie." His mom bobs her head and presses a tissue to her lips when he spins and starts walking away. Martin's there with a hug at the ready.

Layla's lips wobble and she sucks in a ragged breath. Finn kisses the top of her head and gives her shoulder a squeeze. Tori's eyes are glistening too. I swear, if Sammy starts crying, I'm going to lose it.

Tears have never sat well with me. I need to make a joke, do something to break this tension.

"Oh, hey, I nearly forgot!" Mack spins and yells at me from the security checkpoint.

I let go of Sammy's hand and walk towards him. With a

grin, he flicks something into the air. I jump to catch it, opening my hand with a surprise.

"Look after her for me." He points at my chest. "Not a scratch."

I snicker and squeeze his car keys in my palm. "You have my word, man."

"I'll be coming back to check on my baby."

"You better." I laugh, flicking the keys up and catching them again.

With a final wave, he moves through the checkpoint and I lose sight of him. Shoving the keys in my pocket with a heavy sigh, I keep staring at the gate, unable to move until long, slender arms weave around my waist.

Sammy's lips brush the back of my neck before she rests her chin on my shoulder.

"Can't believe he gave you the Camaro. That boy be crazy stupid."

I feel the smile rising on her lips and turn so I can get a better look at it. Her blue eyes sparkle as I wrap my arms around her waist and smirk. "Think of all the fun we can have in a Camaro."

"In the backseat." She winks and bites her tongue between her teeth.

I slap my hand over my heart and practically groan the words, "Oh, man, I love the way you think."

She laughs and tips her head sideways, indicating the sniffling lot behind us. "Should we take these crybabies back to Nelson and remind them that fun can still be had without the Big Mahoney?"

I give her a sad smile. "It won't be the same, though."

"No." She shakes her head. "It won't. But that doesn't mean it's gonna suck, either."

Her wide mouth stretches into a smile as she glides her hands up my arms and wraps them around my neck. "Layla's got Finn. Colt's got Tori. And you've"—she pecks my lips—"got me."

I grin and stretch forward, capturing her mouth again. As her tongue slides against mine, I realize how right she is. Yeah, we're all going to miss Mack, but new things await. For the first time in my life, I'm going into a summer break with a girlfriend...and not just any girlfriend, but the best one out there. My best friend. The one girl who can put up with my shit and still come out smiling.

We've been together for just over a month now and my *there's a chance I might love you* has quickly morphed to an *I'm gone for this girl.* Being with her is easy, fun...natural. Next week, we'll be leaving for Myrtle Beach—two weeks of sun and surf with my family. Sammy's already part of it, and I can't wait to see her in the bikini Layla convinced her to buy last weekend.

With a triumphant grin, I turn towards my friends. Sammy's arm is around my waist, right where it should be. Funny how much things can change in a year. Tori's one of us now, Finn's fallen for the last girl I thought he would, and I'm with Skater Girl.

Tapping her knuckles against Layla's shoulder, Sammy gives her a smile and says, "Come on, you little sissy, let's go back to Nelson and show these jerks how to play some football."

Layla giggles while Colt and Finn make scoffing noises and start ribbing Sammy. I just grin and wrap my arm around her neck, pulling her into a playful headlock. She laughs while I kiss the top of her head and start walking for Mack's car.

Can't believe he's letting me use it while he's away.

I swear to myself that I'll take the honor seriously as I step into the summer sunlight and enjoy the fact that the end of something awesome has dawned the beginning of something epic.

I don't need to prove myself to anyone anymore. I don't need to play the hero or dodge shadows. I'm happy just to be the goofball who loves my family and makes my girlfriend laugh.

Senior year for Sammy, Layla, and me is gonna be just fine.

But first things first…summer vacation.

The perfect way to start something new.

———

Thank you so much for reading Shoot The Gap. I hope you enjoyed it. It was an absolute pleasure to write. If you'd like to show me some support, I'd love for you to leave a review. This is a great way to validate the book and to let other people know what you thought of Tyler and Sammy's story.

If you'd like to see where these characters end up a year from the end of Shoot the Gap, feel free to check out:

THE BIG PLAY JOURNAL

A special addition to the Big Play Novel series...

This journal is filled with images, quotes and special moments from the books. Jordan has written some personal notes of thoughts she had while writing the series, plus (because so many readers asked for it) she's included a snapshot of each couple one year after the Nelson High Raiders novels finished.

NOTE FROM THE AUTHOR

Writing the last book in a series is always bittersweet. You fall in love with the characters you've created, and saying goodbye to them is really hard! I never expected to fall so hard for these Nelson High students, but they won me over in a heartbeat.

When I started these books, I didn't know if Tyler would get his own story. I had set outlines for Colt, Mack and Finn, but Tyler… I wasn't sure. But as I was planning *The Red Zone*, Sammy came to life and she ended up being the perfect match for Tyler. As the idea of them together blossomed in my head, the story expanded to incorporate them more fully, and so the Roxy mystery was born. I'm so grateful. I feel like Sammy and Tyler strengthened this entire series, and I can't imagine the books without them as key characters.

I have to be honest and admit that this was the hardest book of the four to write. Trying to nail that Roxy mystery and also get the romance right for a couple of people who are best buds was really challenging. Sammy's such a tough chick. She doesn't need some guy to rescue or protect her. Trying to find the romance in their friendly banter proved challenging...and *so* rewarding. Sammy and Tyler are great together, and I love that they finally figured it out and found the courage to admit the truth.

If I want readers to take anything away from these books, it's that being true to yourself is always the best bet. You are an amazing, wonderful person, and you shouldn't be afraid to express yourself in a way that makes you feel confident and comfortable. Honesty and truth will always prevail, and if people have a problem with that...they can stick it, right?
LOL :)

Anyway, on to my thank yous...
Rae, Cassie, & Beth, you make my writing life so incredibly enjoyable. I love interacting with you and taking your advice to make these stories what they are. I couldn't do this without you guys, and I hope you all know how much I love and appreciate you.

Same goes for my proofreaders and advanced reader team. You guys are seriously the best. You make my books publishable, and you always make my day when I read your awesome reviews. Interacting with you and chatting about the Nelson High characters has been such a highlight for me.

To all my readers, newsletter subscribers, and social media followers, thank you for supporting my work and helping me continue in my dream job.

To my cover designer, Emily. Thank you for designing a set of AMAZING covers. I love them so much :)

And as always, I have to thank my family who are such great cheerleaders…and my Heavenly Father, who created me to be just who I am and continues to love me unconditionally.

If you'd like to check out my next series, then keep reading. I'm SO excited about these ones. I came up with the idea when I was sixteen years old and it's been percolating ever since—growing, changing, and turning into a trilogy I cannot wait for you to read!

xx

Jordan

THE BROTHERHOOD TRILOGY

Jordan's Brotherhood Trilogy is a romantic suspense series that follows three best friends and the different girls who are pulled into their lives, bringing with them various dangers, a whole lot of feels and numerous chances for these "brothers" to become men.

If you'd like to find out more about the first book—SEE NO EVIL—you can watch the book trailer on YouTube.

SEE NO EVIL BOOK TRAILER.

https://youtu.be/Rv-vCdb0xmc

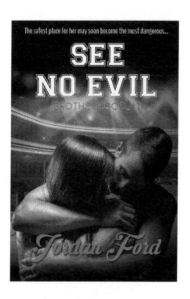

She's a key witness in hiding. He's a hockey player in the room next door. Falling in love would be a dangerous move...but once he learns the truth, how can they resist?

Christiana's friend is dead...and she knows who did it. Now a key witness in a murder trial, she's been hidden away in the one place no one will think to look for her: Eton Preparatory School for Boys.

It's a stupid move. Insane. But she doesn't have a choice.

Instead of completing her senior year with the popular crowd, she's being forced to hide in a school with exactly zero XX chromosomes. Even worse, she's somehow supposed to act like the Neanderthals walking the halls.

But then she meets the guys next door—the smoking-hot ones. And it doesn't help that one in particular could unravel her in a heartbeat...and potentially blow her cover. How's she supposed to resist Trey Calloway, the star hockey player who never backs down from a fight...and who never takes no for an answer?

She's supposed to be focused on staying safe, not on the guy who's getting under her skin.
Her chilling past isn't going to suddenly disappear.
In fact, it might just be catching up with her.

If you're looking for a fast-paced thrill ride packed with drama, suspense, romance and unexpected twists, then See No Evil is just the book for you.

See No Evil is available on Amazon.

BOOKS BY JORDAN FORD

NELSON HIGH RAIDERS NOVELS

The Playmaker

The Red Zone

The Handoff

Shoot The Gap

THE BROTHERHOOD TRILOGY

See No Evil

Speak No Evil

Hear No Evil

BARLOW SISTERS TRILOGY

Curveball

Strike Out

Foul Play

RYDER BAY NOVELS

Over the Falls

The Impact Zone

Face of the Wave

Riptide (novella)

Wipeout

White Water (novella)

FAIRYTALE TWISTS NOVELS

Paper Cranes

You can find information for the next Jordan Ford book release on her WEBSITE.

ABOUT THE AUTHOR

Jordan Ford is a pen name of Melissa Pearl. She is a New Zealand author who has spent her life traveling with her family, attending international schools, and growing up in a variety of cultures. Although it was sometimes hard shifting between schools and lifestyles, she doesn't regret it for a moment. Her experiences have enriched her life and given her amazing insights into the human race.

She believes that everyone has a back story...and that story is fundamental in how people cope and react to life around them. Telling stories that are filled with heartfelt emotion and realistic characters is an absolute passion of Jordan's. Since her earliest memories, she has been making up tales to entertain herself. It wasn't until she reached her teen years that she first considered writing one. A computer failure and lost files put a major glitch in her journey, and it took until she graduated university with a teaching degree before she took up the dream once more. Since then, she hasn't been able to stop.

"Writing high school romances brings me the greatest joy. My heart bubbles, my insides zing, and I am at my happiest when immersed in a great scene with characters who have become real to me."

CONNECT WITH THE AUTHOR

Jordan Ford loves to hear from her readers. Please feel free to contact her through any of the following:

Website:
www.melissapearlauthor.com/page/jordan-ford

Facebook:
www.facebook.com/jordanfordbooks

Instagram:
www.instagram.com/jordanfordbooks